**I must be getting close to the truth if someone was trying to kill me…**

The book had fallen to the floor when the street noise awakened me. A car was racing its engine outside on the street. I remembered my days of fast cars and loud engines. Some things never changed. I had been in such a deep sleep it took a moment for me to come completely awake. I shook my head to clear the cobwebs and looked at the clock on the DVD player. As usual, it was blinking twelve o'clock. I picked up the book, placed it back on the table, and turned off the lamp I had used to read and ultimately used for a night light. When I looked at my watch, I saw it was time to go get Leigh. I walked to my front door and opened it.

The first shot ripped into the doorframe as I was about to exit. My first reaction was to drop. It might have been a lifesaving response, since as I dropped, I heard the CRACK as the second round passed overhead and through the center of the open doorway. If I had been still standing there, I was sure it would have been just as likely to pass through my middle. I rolled to the side of the steps leading to the street and dropped to the ground. My first thought was that I had a pistol and I could have returned the fire, except for one little problem. My gun was in a drawer in my apartment, and I was groveling around on the ground outside.

Retired army officer and former military policeman, "Max" Maxwell, lives and works in a suburb of Seattle, Washington, where he settled down to open a private investigation business. When a SCUBA diving buddy, who is also a teacher and counselor at the local high school, dies in a diving mishap, Max does not accept the verdict of an accidental drowning and digs into the death. What he finds is that his friend led a secret life—one that, if revealed, will shake the very foundations of the school and the community. As Max gets closer to the truth, he discovers that he knows too much about some parts of his new hometown and much too little about others...

# KUDOS for *Dancing in the Dark*

In *Dancing in the Dark* by Paul Sinor, Max Maxwell is a private detective in the Puget Sound area in Washington State, as well as a SCUBA diver. When a friend is killed in a diving accident, Max is hired by the widow to find out if it was an accident or a murder. As Max begins to investigate, he soon discovers that his friend wasn't the good, upstanding citizen everyone thought he was. In fact, he had a secret life with a dark side. Drawn into the world of kinky sex and alternate life styles, Max struggles to find the truth without getting...distracted—or killed. Told from Max's first person POV, the story is tense, intriguing, and fast paced. Mystery fans should love it. ~ *Taylor Jones, Reviewer*

*Dancing in the Dark* by Paul Sinor is the story of a man who is not what he seems to be. Our hero, "Max" Maxwell, is a private detective in northwest Washington. Max is hired to investigate the drowning accident of a fellow SCUBA diver, Jeff Payton a local high-school coach and counselor who, Max, discovers he didn't know as well as he thought. There are a lot of people who might have wanted Jeff dead, though not all of them could have rigged a SCUBA accident. As Max digs for the truth, he learns that Jeff wasn't the man Max thought he was. In fact, he wasn't a nice man at all. Still, not everyone with a motive has the skill and knowledge to make a murder look like a diving accident. And those who could seem to have alibis—or do they? Sinor has crafted an intriguing mystery set in an exciting world of danger and adventure, with plenty of action and interesting characters. It's a well-written tale with a surprising ending—one you'll have a hard time putting down. ~ *Regan Murphy, Reviewer*

# ACKNOWLEDGEMENTS

Writing a novel is not a solitary endeavor. It is the culmination of a lot of work by a lot of people, many of whom go unrecognized and probably unappreciated for their efforts in bringing a work such as this to life. I have many to thank, and I know I will not name them all, but I want to especially thank the entire team at Black Opal Books for not only taking a chance on this book, but on the outstanding job they did in the editing and on the cover. For those who read this book and find mistakes, no matter what they are, they are mine and mine alone. Even with the best editors, proofreaders, and spell check programs available, mistakes do happen, so if/when you find one, blame me. I owe a special thanks to several of my writer friends who read this manuscript in its infancy and suggested improvements. To Annette, Doc, Mike, Joe, and especially to my wife Jewell, I could not have done this without all of you.

# DANCING IN THE DARK

PAUL SINOR

*A Black Opal Books Publication*

GENRE: MYSTERY-DETECTIVE/CRIME THRILLER

This is a work of fiction. Names, places, characters and incidents are either the product of the author's imagination or are used fictitiously, and any resemblance to any actual persons, living or dead, businesses, organizations, events or locales is entirely coincidental. All trademarks, service marks, registered trademarks, and registered service marks are the property of their respective owners and are used herein for identification purposes only. The publisher does not have any control over or assume any responsibility for author or third-party websites or their contents.

DANCING IN THE DARK
Copyright © 2017 by Paul Sinor
Cover Design by Jackson Cover Designs
All cover art copyright © 2017
All Rights Reserved
Print ISBN: 978-1-626946-23-1

First Publication: MARCH 2017

All rights reserved under the International and Pan-American Copyright Conventions. No part of this book may be reproduced or transmitted in any form or by any means, electronic or mechanical, including photocopying, recording, or by any information storage and retrieval system, without permission in writing from the publisher.

**WARNING: The unauthorized reproduction or distribution of this copyrighted work is illegal. Criminal copyright infringement, including infringement without monetary gain, is investigated by the FBI and is punishable by up to 5 years in federal prison and a fine of $250,000. Anyone pirating our ebooks will be prosecuted to the fullest extent of the law and may be liable for each individual download resulting therefrom.**

ABOUT THE PRINT VERSION: If you purchased a print version of this book without a cover, you should be aware that the book is stolen property. It was reported as "unsold and destroyed" to the publisher, and neither the author nor the publisher has received any payment for this "stripped book."

IF YOU FIND AN EBOOK OR PRINT VERSION OF THIS BOOK BEING SOLD OR SHARED ILLEGALLY, PLEASE REPORT IT TO: lpn@blackopalbooks.com

Published by Black Opal Books **http://www.blackopalbooks.com**

DEDICATION

*For my two daughters, Colleen and Victoria.
Nothing more needs to be said.*

# Chapter 1

I was returning from a two-day visit with Bill Ward, an old army buddy of mine across the Puget Sound in Kingston, Washington, a city not far from Seattle. I got to Bill's place about once a year. We spent the time drinking too much, fishing too little, and telling too many war stories we both knew were bullshit. I knew him in Iraq and, when I retired from the army and moved to Edmonds, he was one of the first people I stumbled into. He was sitting at a bar not far from the public fishing pier in town, lamenting about the lack of activity, when I felt his laugh tear loose a memory I thought had been buried for years. His was a laugh you never forget. The last time I heard it, we were in a club in a rear area in Baghdad, trying to out-drink a group of air force pilots who had just arrived and were new to the war zone. I returned to my unit, and he departed a few days later for a life of retirement.

Two years later, I followed his lead and left twenty-plus years in the army behind. Time would show that neither of us could handle retirement very well.

I stood on the forward end of the ferry and watched two emergency response vehicles clear a path to the Edmonds Underwater Park. The water was much too cold for most normal people to use for swimming. It had to be another diving accident.

There was a fine mist of spray coming from the front of the ferry. It was something you got used to if you rode it enough. Another thing you had to get used to was people you did not know starting conversations with you as you stood by the rail.

"Whadda ya think happened?" an old man asked, holding a large paper cup containing one of his probably numerous daily lattes.

"Could be just about anything, I guess. Heart attack maybe." I tried to make it short so he would move on.

"Friend of mine who lives here says the water'll freeze you, even if you're wearing a protective suit." He paused, took a sip of the hot latte, and spoke again with a thin white mustache of milk foam on his upper lip. "You think that's so?"

"I don't think it's quite that bad, but it can get cold in the water."

A crowd had already formed at the rear of the aid vehicles. From the deck of the ferry, I watched the rescue divers enter the water. Down the rail from where I stood a tourist with a pair of binoculars gave us a play-by-play.

"Looks like three, no, two divers going in. One is still on the beach. He's taking off his tanks. There are a couple of cops standing with him."

I learned to dive, compliments of Uncle Sam, during a tour of duty with Special Forces. I liked it and continued to dive, even after leaving the Forces and retiring from the army. The Underwater Park provided an excellent place to dive and to send friends who occasionally dropped in on me.

When the ferry docked, I returned to my SUV, got in, and waited till it was my turn to leave. As I joined the line of almost two hundred cars leaving the ferry, I instinctively turned left and drove slowly by the activity to see what was happening with the divers.

There were more rubber-neckers per capita in the Seattle area than any place in America. A car with a flat tire on the side of I-5 would slow traffic for miles. I couldn't complain too much as I added to the congestion around the emergency vehicles.

As I passed, I saw a gurney with a sheet-covered body on it being loaded into the back of the ambulance. It was another victim of too little training, or too much confidence, or just plain bad luck. Either way, dead was dead. A second diver sat with a blanket around him, or perhaps her. At least the victim had been diving with a buddy and hadn't died alone.

I drove up the hill and passed through the center of town, all three blocks of it. It was small but it suited my purposes.

Several years earlier, I spent twenty-four months in the area on recruiting duty with the army. I liked it and, when it came time to retire, Edmonds was in the top five cities on my list of places to live. The final decision was one I left to my daughters. My oldest had already started college, so her choice was staying in North Carolina or moving with the family. She chose door number two, and transferred to the University of Washington. The youngest one completed high school once we arrived and got accepted at Tulane in New Orleans. The next year my wife told me how she felt about some of my bad habits, got half my retirement pay in the divorce settlement, and I found myself alone in Puget Sound with the rest of my life ahead of me.

A couple of times in the army, the bad guys used me to qualify for their marksmanship badges. The VA was somewhat benevolent, so I received a monthly disability check. Since it was for a disability and not considered income, it was not a part of the divorce settlement, and I got to keep all of it. Because of the disability, my daughters qualified for student grants and all sorts of financial aid, so I could just about make it on what my wife left me. It's the "just about" part that caused me to look for something to do when I retired. That something to do turned out to be hanging a shingle out as a private investigator. I spent seven years in the army's Military Police Corps, so I met the state requirements for a license. I didn't get the glamorous cases. I'd been offered a few but, unlike most other people in the business and all of the ones on television, I knew how it felt to get shot. It was no fun, so I stuck to divorces, missing and unfaithful husbands, and equally unfaithful wives. I occasionally did some background investigations on a contract basis for the government.

My office was nothing to write home about. It was in an old building that was once a pharmacy. I used the main space for my office and the upstairs for an occasional place to sleep. I had everything but a shower on the second floor. I solved that little inconvenience when I met Leigh Hayes. She worked as a hostess at one of Edmond's better restaurants. She had a condo downtown, compliments of her divorce settlement, and it had a very nice shower.

The first ambulance passed me just as I rolled off the end of the ferry and crossed over the dock and onto the city street. I could see in my rearview mirror two more EMT vehicles that were still by the waterfront park. Several police cruisers lined the street and one pumper from the fire station was on the scene. Before I got to my office, I heard the wail of the siren as the second one took off on its way to either the local trauma center or the dive chamber. If a diver came out of the Sound with the bends, he or she would be quickly rushed to the decompression chamber at the University Hospital. I had been in the underwater park several times, and the depth there was not great enough to cause any real damage. If it was the bends, the divers had been farther out in the Sound or done something stupid. After a couple of dives in the park, I failed to see the fascination of diving in what amounted to a pool of murky, dark, extremely cold water. When I got my certification, I found out I really liked diving so I spent a lot of my leisure time underwater. I'd even been in some areas as bad as in the Sound, but it was required training in the army. For pleasure, I'd dive in Hawaii or Key West or some of the smaller Pacific Islands where you could still see wrecks of Japanese Zeros and army tanks that didn't make it ashore. Diving was a lot of fun but it also required a lot of work. I was finding as I passed each new birthday, I paid much more attention to my pain/gain equations.

I pulled into my parking space, walked to the front of my building, and unlocked the door. Across the street, two women were picking up a drink from one of the many latte carts that were as abundant in the Pacific Northwest as fire hydrants in a normal city. I once worked for a lady who was trying to find out how much her husband was making on two carts. It was for a divorce, so he low-balled her. After watching him for two weeks, my conservative estimate was eighty thousand a year from each one. Latte as a business was second only to Microsoft and Boeing in Seattle.

There was a stack of mail on the floor under the mail drop in my front door. Some of it folded under the door as I pushed it open. My answering machine was blinking. I didn't count the blinks but I had several messages. I turned on the light by my desk, took off my windbreaker, and sat down.

I kept meaning to upgrade to the internal system offered by my phone company but I never seem to get around to it. Leigh said I lived so far in the past I still looked for eight-tracks and Beta movies at the rental store.

I opened the first piece of mail and pushed the button on the machine. After a few seconds of rewinding, the first message came out. I must have hit the volume switch by mistake because the sound was so loud I could even hear it in my deaf ear. I quickly turned it down and listened to a message from someone selling tickets to a charity circus. The next message was much better. It was Leigh.

"Are we alone?" She had a way of lowering her voice so it snaked its way up from deep within her libido and completely bypassed the voice box. She did this most effectively late at night on the phone. "I just got off work. It's nearly three a.m. If you were here, do you know what I'd do to you?"

It was instinct that made me look around the empty office to make certain I was alone as she told me the things she had in mind. When she finished, I looked to see if the machine was smoking a cigarette.

The remainder of my messages were an assortment ranging from two more tele-marketing calls to a family looking for a daughter they thought might be working as a prostitute on Aurora Avenue, the main street for hookers in Seattle. My mail was no less fulfilling, so fifteen minutes after I arrived, I was open for business.

I could see outside my office through a large plate glass window. It overlooked nothing more than a city street. If I went to the corner of the room, I could see the ferry dock, the Sound, and the snow-covered mountains of the peninsula standing guard over the far western final bit of land in the state. Not only could I see all this, but I could also keep an eye on Crazy George.

In earlier less politically correct times, Crazy George would have been referred to as the Village Idiot. Today he was regarded by those who didn't know him as simply an emotionally and residentially challenged citizen of the city. He spent a lot of time walking around the statue at the town square and talking to the pigeons. He also came by on occasion and talked to me.

I was standing by the window when he came up the sidewalk toward my office.

He opened the door, stuck his head cautiously inside, looked around, then entered. "Afternoon, Colonel. You been gone a couple of days this time, huh?"

"Come on in, George." I knew it was useless to try to keep him out. Once he saw the office was empty, he knew I was good for a little conversation and a few bucks. "I don't have any coffee yet, but if you'll fly, I'll buy." I handed him a five-dollar bill with the intent of having him go across the street and get two cups of coffee.

"I'll do just that, Colonel. In just a minute." George carefully folded the money and put it in the pocket of the old army field jacket he always wore. Once the bill was tucked away, I knew I'd never see the coffee or the change. "Was you down by the ferry dock this afternoon?" he asked.

He picked up a newspaper, folded it, and placed it on the edge of the windowsill. George took a seat on the folded paper and looked around the office as if he'd never been in it before.

"I came in on the ferry about thirty minutes ago. I saw the activity and I drove by it. I couldn't tell much, though."

George nodded toward a calendar I had placed over the table where I had my coffee pot. "That a new picture, Colonel? Looks like one of them pictures I seen in the library down in Seattle." He stared at the large photograph of a herd of buffalo in the snow of Yellowstone Park.

I formally met George at the Veterans Hospital one day about a year ago. As a veteran, I had to go in once a year for a check up to determine if anything I lost in the army has grown back or healed itself. In my case, it was my hearing. I spent too many nights on a firebase with a 105 Howitzer nestled next to my pillow. I was sitting in a waiting room when a Black man settled into the chair beside me. As soon as he sat down, he began a conversation with me as if we had been friends for years. If memory served me, he started in the middle of a dissertation about the Mariners and how they were one of the worst teams in the major leagues.

"Yes, sir, Colonel, them Mariners ought to be playin' against some little league team somewhere. Only I don't think no little fellers want to embarrass the Mariners by beatin' 'em."

The next time I saw him, he was breaking down cardboard boxes behind the building next to mine. He recognized me, and since then, he'd been dropping by on occasion.

George had been a draftee during the Viet Nam war. After a quick couple of months training, he, like so many other young men, were sent to Viet Nam to grow up overnight. I had seen hundreds of men just like George during my time in the army. I came in after Viet Nam, but there were many draftees who lived through their tour of duty in the jungle and found a home in the army. I felt from day one that we had done many of them a disservice by training them and then returning them to the world after twelve months in Hell.

We still heard about people, like George, who didn't adjust to civilian life when they got on the six o'clock news with a rifle in their hand and a massacre at their feet.

Since George made no effort to leave for our coffee, I stepped over to the table where I kept my coffee maker and began to make a pot. The bottom of the glass pot in my coffee maker had been burned so many times it was as black as the coffee that flowed into it from the machine.

George reached into his jacket pocket, and pulled out a bottle with about two inches of God-knows-what in the bottom. "I got just about enough for a touch for both of us, lessen' you got a big thirst, Colonel"

I eyed the liquid. The label was missing from the bottle. Not a good sign. I hated to turn down a drink, but even I had a few standards. Drinking with George from a bottle without a label could only mean one of two things. George was keeping his favorite bottle and filling it with whatever he could find, or he was making his own. I was already partially deaf. I couldn't take a chance on adding blind to my list.

"It's a little early for me, George, but you go ahead."

Without waiting, he poured the contents of the bottle into a large mug, filled it half way with coffee and began to sip slowly.

"Looked real bad down to the park. I seen the amb'lances coming so I walked over to see what they was doing. By the time I got up there, they was pulling a man out of the water. He was already dead. They was trying to do that breathin' thang for him, but I seen enough people who done give up the ghost to know a dead man when I see one." George took a long pull from the mug and slipped away to revisit some of the ghosts he had tucked away. For a minute, he just stared straight ahead. Someone once called it a two-thousand-yard stare. For George, the stare probed for miles, not yards.

"I seen him and that other young feller that was with him before. I don't think the boy was hurt too bad. They had him on a stretcher, but he was fightin' them men trying to put him in that amb'lance."

"You know who they were?"

George spent most of his time walking around town, so it was quite possible he did know the victims.

"I worked over at the high school a couple of times. I used to watch 'em play football. The dead one was the coach. The boy looked like the quarterback from a couple of years ago. I could be wrong, though. They both had on them black frogman suits."

I looked beyond George and watched the traffic on Main Street. My thoughts drifted back to a man I met when my daughter was a senior in the high school. Jeff Payton had been her counselor. He seemed to take a real interest in the kids. He was also the man who led the football team to the state championship game. He and I went diving several times. I first saw him at the dive shop. We took a Saturday afternoon and went over to Whidbey Island. After that, we went to the Underwater Park on occasion and spent a weekend in the San Juan Islands last year. Coach Jeff Payton.

And now Crazy George was sitting in my office, drinking my coffee and telling me an old friend was dead.

# Chapter 2

When George finished his coffee, he took the cup to the back room, rinsed it, and placed it on the counter next to the sink. He said something when he walked by me on the way out, but I did not hear it plainly enough to respond. My mind was elsewhere. George knew it and forgave me my not answering him.

I called the Edmonds Police Department and asked if they had identified the person killed in the diving accident. I got the answer I expected and deserved. No public information, pending notification of next of kin. I did not envy the officer that job.

I wondered if George and I were the only two people who knew Jeff was dead. I wondered where his wife Tracy was at this very moment. When she heard the news it would be a minute in time which would forever remain fixed in her mind. She would always know exactly where she was and what she was doing when she was notified of Jeff's death.

I wanted to call her and offer my condolences. If she hadn't been notified I did not want to be a part of that forever-fixed memory, so I did the next best thing. Nothing. I looked at my watch. Only seven hours until I could meet Leigh.

We usually met after she got off from work. Every time I did it meant I either had to stay up practically all night or grab a quick nap. With nothing else to do, I went home and read a book until I fell asleep on the couch. When I took a nap, I'd set my alarm for one a.m. and drive down to the restaurant. By the time I got there, she would be coming out of the place. With few options of things to do or places to go, we usually went straight back to her condo. Sometimes we'd just talk, sometimes it was breakfast, and sometimes we couldn't wait to jump each other's bones. I tried to anticipate which it would be but I never knew in advance.

Leigh was three inches shorter than my five eleven. When she worked, she wore heels, a long black skirt, and a white blouse. With her heels on, we stood nose-to-nose. She had hair that was too dark not to have some help, but that was something I was smart enough not to mention. She had features that indicated her father's Italian lineage. Her olive skin looked especially sensuous in the moonlight.

I parked, crossed the parking lot, and met one of the lot attendants. "Evening, Max. You picking up Leigh, or you going in for a late one?"

"You know I never drink till I've been awake at least an hour. I'll have one later on."

The building had a dining room that faced the yachts moored at the city docks. Leigh and I'd been on a few of them as guests, but a yacht was something I never wanted to own. Most of the ones I could see were like some of the women a few of my friends were married to or had on their arms at parties. They were great to look at, but too expensive for my blood. Many of the sailboats were new. Their owners had collected a huge insurance settlement several years earlier when a freak snowstorm collapsed the metal roofs over the boats, sending over one hundred of them to the bottom of the basin. Some owners looked at it as a God-send when they surveyed the damage. They took the money and ran.

I was standing by the window watching the moonlight flash like iridescence on the dark water when Leigh came up beside me.

"I'll be ready in a minute. I've got to get my jacket." She gave me a fleeting kiss on the cheek and sped away.

Roger, the bartender, was still checking up. "Hey, Max. What's happin'?" He placed the last few bottles on the cart he was loading and began to push it my way. "You hear about Coach Payton? Somebody said he and a couple of kids drowned down at the park today. You know anything about it?"

"Yeah." I knew and I also knew I didn't want to talk about it. When I didn't answer, he continued with his work. I watched as he pushed the cart pass me and toward the open liquor closet.

"Bad enough it had to be him, but if any of the kids died with him…" His voice trailed off. "That'd really be a bitch."

Leigh came up, slid her arm around mine, and guided me toward the door. "You guys can talk tomorrow. I want to go home now."

We crossed the room and pushed the button for the elevator.

Before it came, Roger yelled across to us. "Hey, Leigh, it's already tomorrow." He was laughing at his own joke when the elevator door opened.

In the parking lot, we walked straight to her car. We had previously made an agreement that anytime we had to leave a car, it would be mine. There were fewer car thieves interested in Toyota Four Runners than in red Miata's. Mine would be a lot safer sitting in the port parking lot overnight than hers.

She handed me the keys. "You drive. I'll never make it tonight. I'm beat." She pulled her dress to mid-thigh and slid into the seat. She saw me obviously admiring her legs. "Down, big fellow. I'll give you a rain check when we get home."

I think she was asleep before I even got the car started.

When we got to her place, I parked and watched her sleep for a few moments. I reached over and gently touched her cheek. Her first reaction was to move ever so slightly and continue to sleep. I hated to do it, but I called her name until she awakened.

"Time to go inside, Sleeping Beauty." I said as I opened the car door and the interior filled with light.

"Light's gotta die," she said sleepily.

I laughed and tried to help her out while she kept her eyes closed.

She leaned against the doorframe at her front door while I fumbled with the lock. When I finally got the door open, she smiled, gave me a kiss, and disappeared inside. That was my not so subtle indication that I was on my own. I closed her door and went home. I would worry about the logistics of getting her car to her and mine back tomorrow.

The local newspaper was a weekly so it took several more days for the story of Jeff's death to make the front pages in Edmonds. The paper published the feature the same day as the funeral. The first two pages of the small edition read like a memorial issue. The *Seattle Post Intelligencer* had a small piece on Jeff the morning after it happened, but even the accidental death of someone like Jeff took second place to a drive-by shooting in the Central District. I thought they did a good job of comparing the difference between the turnouts for his memorial service at the high school with the seeming lack of interest for those killed in some of the other areas of the community.

I didn't do funerals, so Leigh and I paid our respects at the graveside service. Jeff was a veteran so he had a flag and a bugler. It was the ROTC detachment from the school and they did an admirable job. Very few who attended were the same after the last note of "Taps" drifted across the Sound. We had all lost a little. It may have been a family member, a teacher, coach, or friend. But we shared the loss, if for just a moment in the afternoon sun.

Jeff was married but he had no children. I thought that was why he was such a success at school. He treated each kid like they were one of his own.

I saw Tracy Payton standing with a small group of students, consoling them. Leigh took me by the arm and led me toward Tracy. "Don't you think you should say something to her?"

Tracy saw us and smiled. It was much more than I could have done under the circumstances, I was certain. "Max—" She extended her hand. "—it's so good of you to come."

"Tracy—" I stammered, not even knowing how to finish the sentence.

"Jeff always liked the diving trips you and he took. I think he just wanted to listen to you tell stories about the army. He said you were good at it."

"Yeah, I guess I did tell a lot of war stories when we went. But I never claimed they were all true."

Tracy laughed a little. It made me feel good. "Oh, he knew that. It's just that you were different from most of the people he knew. Jeff said he didn't even know anyone else except the advisors from the ROTC unit at school who were in combat. And being a private investigator—"

Leigh came to my rescue. She leaned over, gave Tracy a hug, and whispered something in her ear. It must have been effective. Tracy gave her a smile and returned her attention to the kids standing around her.

We were on the way home before Leigh spoke. "Did you call Vicki and tell her Jeff was dead? Didn't you tell me he had been one of her counselors when she was in school here?"

"I'll tell her on Friday. You know she always calls around three."

"And always needs money for something," she added with a bite. She hesitated as she thought about what she had just said. "At least she can still talk to you. By the time I was nineteen, my father and I hadn't spoken for two years."

There had been times right after the divorce when I didn't think I would ever be able to speak to either of my girls again. Maybe it was the whole package. Maybe it was just the part I was responsible for, but, when their mother announced she was leaving, I was immediately cast as the bad guy. In a way, I guess I was. But I wasn't the one leaving. It took a while for that to settle in. After that, Vicki and I seemed to develop more of a friendly relationship. It was not so much that of a father and daughter but almost like business associates. At twenty-three, her older sister had already broken most of the family ties, so it was not so rough on her.

By the time I dropped Leigh off at her place and got back to my office, it was almost four. I had two letters on the floor underneath the mail slot, and the message light on my machine was blinking. The first one was from a woman wanting me to investigate someone using her name and social security number to cash checks on a bank account she had closed in Oregon. I made a note to call the district attorney to see who was liable in a situation like that before calling her back.

The second call was much more interesting. It too

was a female voice but much younger. "I know you were a friend of Mister Payton's. And I know you went diving with him sometimes. Did he seem like the kind of diver who would drown? Maybe you want to ask around about—" Her voice faltered. I heard her stifle a sob. "Ask about some of the counseling he was doing. Especially down in Po—"

"Dammit!" I slammed my fist down on my desk. I only had a thirty second tape on my machine, and it had ended before she finished what she was saying. I immediately pushed the replay button and listened again.

After listening three times, I pulled a small tape recorder from the bottom drawer of my desk and recorded the message onto a new tape. I might not have all of it, but I would have a permanent copy of the portion I did have.

I made myself a note to sign up for the answering service with the phone company.

# Chapter 3

Sometimes, especially when I was alone, I wondered why Leigh continued to accept some of my behaviors. Two days after Jeff's funeral, she had a day off. I picked her up at her condo, and we went to an early dinner and a movie. The movie was one she picked. We usually took turns and this was my payback for the last time I took her to a film that was long on action and short on plot. I managed to remember enough of this one to actually discuss it with her when we left the theater.

By the time we got to the restaurant and finished our first drink, I had already embarrassed her by giving my admittedly right-wing opinion about the relationship between street crime and minorities to a man seated beside us at the bar. By the time the guy, whose name I never knew, started quoting stats to back up our individual side of the arguments, the manager was ready to call the cops or throw us out.

Only quick intervention by Leigh saved me. I knew we would discuss it on the drive home.

"I thought you and the man at the bar were going to go out in the alley," she said from the dark silence enveloping her side of the car.

"He was safe. I don't think I wanted to get into any

dark place with him. No telling what I might walk away with."

The traffic on I-5 was backing up, even though rush hour had been over for hours. After a few minutes of creeping along at fifteen miles or less per hour, we passed the trouble spot. It was a cop giving a roadside sobriety test to a man who was way past the need for the test. Like everyone else on the freeway, I down shifted the little red convertible and pulled up close to the car ahead of us so Leigh and I could rubberneck.

"Sometimes I wonder if you really believe all this crap you try to feed everyone, or if you do it for some sort of shock effect. You know. An image thing," she said, not so much to me, but to see how the words sound.

I knew the slow traffic had given her time to mentally replay the tapes of my confrontation with the man in the bar. I also knew enough not to respond.

Earlier, I had left the Toyota at her place. When we got there, it was late so I kissed her goodnight, changed to my SUV, and drove myself home. Between the half of my retirement my wife's lawyer let me keep, my disability pay, and the money I made working, I managed to live almost like I wanted. I lived in a duplex in a group of four similar units overlooking the waterfront. It was much nicer than when I attempted to live and work in my office. I had a place with a view of both the Puget Sound and the mountains to the north. I could see Mt. Baker on the Canadian border and the even-more-majestic mountains across the Sound on the Olympic Peninsula. In other places, views like that cost more than a retired army snake-eater could even comprehend.

I furnished my place modestly, but it was with things I liked. I didn't have to ask permission to buy a large television and a small stereo. My couch was comfortable. It was purchased separately from the large chair across from it, so the match was for feel and not color. I had a couple of prints on the wall I bought on a trip to Gettysburg. Few people who saw them even recognized General Lee. The Civil War was not one of the more discussed topics in the Pacific Northwest.

My bedroom contained the king-sized bed and other furnishings I managed to successfully negotiate for in the divorce. This room was dictated by the size of the bed, as all future apartments would be, as long as I owned the bedroom set.

When I got home, I slid easily into the still unmade bed. I tried to make it each morning when I left, but sometime it took a backseat to reading the paper or taking out the garbage. I was asleep within a few minutes. I had just enough to drink to keep me asleep almost all night. My internal alarm played "Reveille" each morning around five. As soon as my eyes opened in the morning, I was wide awake. It made my wife crazy when I'd jump out of bed as soon as the alarm went off. Ten minutes later, I was in the shower.

If I wasn't in the mood to cook, I usually went to the Treetopper Cafe for breakfast. The Treetopper was the kind of cafe where legends were made. It was open all night. It had an adjoining bar that was closed only from two until six a.m. The Treetop held its own with some of the bigger places in town. It was nestled between two used car lots on Aurora Avenue. The place had probably been many things in the life of the building. If seen from the outside for the first time, you would think it was a knife and gun club. Once inside the door, there was no doubt. Only the waitresses had more tattoos than the cooks. The booths were vinyl covered with material that was broken, split, and cut in so many places the owners had stopped trying to put tape patches on the seats. The floors were sticky and a sign over the counter announced

*SMOKING IS ALLOWED AND ENCOURAGED. TO HELL WITH THE CITY!* The ham and cheese and jalapeno omelet made it all worthwhile.

After breakfast, I went to the office. I was usually the first one in town to turn on my lights. Most people opened for business at nine or ten. I was always in by eight. Sometimes I actually had something to do.

I was skimming the want ads in the *Post-Intelligencer* when the phone rang. I had my machine set to answer on the third ring, so I picked it up on the second.

"Maxwell, here." Although nobody spoke, I could hear a lot of background noise. It almost sounded like a party. If it was, it must have been one hell of a party to be still going that strong at eight in the morning.

"Hello. If you're there, you'll have to speak up. I can hardly hear you." I tried again. "Hello?"

There was no response. I was still holding the receiver when the caller hung up their end of the phone. Before the caller hung up, I heard a bell ring in the background. At least I knew it wasn't a party.

I had tried to keep the caller on the line but it didn't work. I placed the phone on its cradle and sat at my desk. Calls with no one saying anything were not too unusual in my business. Many people were prepared to call for assistance, but when it came time to actually speak to me or any other investigator, they lost their nerve. It wasn't easy to tell a stranger your problem and then ask them for help. I dismissed the call as someone with cold feet or a change of heart and let it go.

My mind turned to Jeff Payton as I poured another cup of coffee.

I tried to think if Jeff had ever said anything about doing any free-lance counseling anywhere other than the school. I couldn't remember any but that was not unusual. We were friends, but not close enough that I would have known something about a second job. I finished the cup of coffee and pulled out an old atlas. I traced by finger down I-5 looking for any city that started with the "Po" sound the caller had left on my machine. The logical choice was Portland, but that was two hundred miles away. Quite a distance for a part time job.

The door to my office made a little squeaking noise when it was opened. It was the squeak that made me look up.

George was standing inside the office. "Don't worry Colonel, it's just me."

"Come on in. There's coffee if you want some." I pointed toward the pot.

He saw the map and came over to my desk. "You goin' on another trip?"

I began folding the map. "No, I was looking for something."

"Find it?"

I ignored his question since I didn't know what I was looking for.

George took his usual seat on the windowsill. "I seen you at Coach Payton's funeral. It was real nice. As far as funerals go, don't you think?"

"I didn't actually go to the service. I was—uh—" I began to stammer. "The best I could do was make it to the cemetery."

"I know." George sat quietly for a moment. I sensed he had more to say, so I waited for him to speak. "You know, it just ain't right."

"What's that, George?"

"The coach gettin' killed like that."

Coming from the man whom I assumed lived most of his adult life on the streets, who worked a variety of jobs, whose background was a source of speculation for most who knew him, not "the coach dying like that, but the coach gettin' killed like that." Made me listen.

"Do you want to tell me something, George?"

"Ain't nothing to tell, 'cept the coach didn't drown. I seen him down there too many times. He knew what he was doing. You went diving with him. How come he didn't drown when you two was together? No, sir, somethin' ain't right."

We sat in silence for a moment. I was trying to think of something to say, to either console him to the fact Coach Payton probably did drown in an unfortunate but likely diving accident, or get him to tell me more of his theory, when the phone rang. I started to let the machine answer, but George looked at me and nodded, almost like he was granting me permission to interrupt our conversation.

I picked it up on the third ring. "Maxwell here. May I help you?" I always answered using my name, rather than the name of the business. I guess it was an old habit from the army. Always identify yourself and know who you are speaking to at all times. When there was no response, I repeated it. I was about to hang up when I heard a female voice.

"I—I didn't expect to get you. I thought I would have to leave a message."

I didn't have to replay the tape in my micro cassette to know this was the same voice from the earlier call. I was fumbling for a small device I used as a combination recorder and phone tap for my own phone. I had to reach around the desk and pull it from one of the cabinets. I finally got the device and activated it. "I didn't get your entire message last time. You were cut off in the middle." I hesitated. "You were telling me I should check on some counseling."

I looked across the room at George. He took one last

pull from his cup and stood. "You think on what I said." He placed the cup on the table and, with the door squeaking, opened it and left. I felt badly but I wanted to give my full attention to the caller. And I thought that attention needed to be alone.

"I saw you at the cemetery. You had the red Miata, didn't you?"

I felt certain the young woman hadn't called to talk about cars but if that's what it took to find out her real reason, I was willing to try it. "Do you have a car?" Although she didn't answer, I could hear her breathing so I knew she was still on the line. I was about to take another approach when she finally spoke.

"How well did you know—uh—Mister Payton?"

"We hadn't known each other for many years, but I did consider him a friend. Why?"

"Maybe if you knew more about him, he—" She hesitated.

"He what?" My caller sounded like a young girl with a lot of pain and some excess baggage that she wanted someone to help her carry.

"Nothing, nothing. I've got to go." As usual she hung up without telling me anything. Or perhaps she had told me more than she realized.

I didn't need to get involved, personally or professionally in the death of Jeff Payton. It was none of my business. I knew it. I told Leigh the same thing at dinner that night.

That was why I went by the police station the next morning and talked to Detective Sergeant Fitzgerald.

I knew Fitz from having worked with him on a missing husband case last year. The wife had called me after her husband's car turned up near the end of a road leading to an old semi-abandoned boathouse at Norma Beach. There was no sign of foul play, no blood, no note, no nothing. The husband was eventually found in Vancouver living with his new lover, the young man who did yard work for the former husband and wife.

The wife hired me to find the husband and, when I did, Fitz finally had to get a restraining order against her. It was fair to say she was not a happy camper.

Fitz was a young detective. He was one of the new and improved versions of law enforcement officers working today. He was first generation and a college graduate. I would not be surprised to see his name on a ballot someday.

The walk from my office to the police department was a short and usually a very pleasant one. In the summer, the city was filled with hanging flower baskets. Pots of more colors and types of flowers than anyone less than a horticulturist could keep up with lined the sidewalks. I couldn't name more than three of the varieties of flowers but even I thought it looked nice.

There were only two people who held a license as a private investigator in Edmonds. Not too many others had offices in the area north of Seattle, so I was not unknown to most of the men and women in the public safety buildings in the county.

Fitzgerald's office was in the rear of the first floor suite of rooms occupied by the all three of the city's detectives. Since he was the senior one in rank he usually worked the day shift. I caught him as he was entering the building.

"Detective Fitzgerald, can I speak to you for a minute?"

In public, I always used his rank when addressing him. Some of the men thought it was a sign of respect. Others recognized it as a holdover from my years in the military, never calling someone by their name and not their rank.

Either way, it was a natural thing to do. Only when we were alone or away from the city buildings did we become Fitz and Max.

"Out here or can I go inside and put up my stuff?" he asked.

"It doesn't matter to me. I just need a couple of minutes."

He made the decision for us as I followed him inside the building.

The police building in Edmonds was co-located with the rest of the City Hall complex. Next to it was the Fire Department. We were almost to his office when the siren outside the building began to wail. A fire truck and rescue vehicle peeled out and headed toward their next crisis.

"Come on in. Want a cup?" Fitzgerald motioned toward a chair in front of his desk and a coffee pot in the corner of the office. He got himself a cup.

"I'll pass," I said as I pulled the chair away from the desk. With a little more space between us, I didn't feel as if I was being interrogated.

He took off the gray coat from a suit that probably cost five hundred or better. His tie was silk and was perfectly tied. He carefully placed the coat on a wood hanger, hung it on a rack behind his door, and looked at me over the rim of his cup as he sipped the warm coffee. "What is it this time? Another runaway husband?"

"Nothing like that. I'm just curious about Jeff Payton."

"Curious? In what way?"

"Jeff and I did a couple of dives together. He was certified as an instructor. I'm just curious as to what he did wrong."

"Who said he did anything wrong?"

"See. That's why I'm curious. The times we went

diving together, we did almost everything alike. I just don't want to make the same mistake he did."

It was the best I could do at the time, and I thought Fitz accepted my explanation.

He went to a file cabinet and pulled a thin report. "The coroner hasn't given his final report to us yet, but it looks like he got caught up in some of the pilings or something at the old dry dock in the underwater park. His tanks got caught and he couldn't get loose. Guess he'd been down too long when it happened. So by the time he figured out he was stuck, he didn't have enough air to get back to the surface. The kid who was with him almost panicked and drowned himself, too. He was no help at all." He closed the file and placed it back in the drawer. "I know you and he were friends, but it looks like he drowned. Plain and simple. That's what the coroners report's gonna say. If he had insurance, it's going to pay double for accidental death. He's leaving a very pretty, and probably very wealthy, widow." He stood in the middle of his office, hands in his pockets. I took that as my signal to leave.

"I really appreciate the info." I started to leave when he moved slightly between me and the door.

"If, by any chance, you think we're not all on the same sheet of music, you will let me know, won't you, Mister Maxwell?"

"I assure you my interest in this is just as a concerned diver." Without waiting for his response, I stepped around him and left his office.

Outside, I ran into Officer Reed, one of the senior men on the police force. Reed was a retired Marine gunnery sergeant, and, like most retirees, he felt a comradeship with others who had spent the better part of their lives in the military service. When he found out I retired as a lieutenant colonel, he seemed to go out of his way to become friends. He always greeted me when we met with my former rank.

"Afternoon, Colonel. What brings you down here?"

"I came down to see Detective Fitzgerald, Gunny. He's working on Coach Payton's drowning."

"That was a shame, wasn't it? He really had a way with the kids. My son played for him three years ago, and both my daughters had him for a counselor, he did a lot for them. They really took it hard when they found out he died."

While he was talking, I couldn't help but think of the young female voice on my recorder.

# CHAPTER 4

I got a copy of the initial report done by the coroner. It was just like Detective Fitzgerald told me in his office. The cause of death was accidental drowning. There were no witnesses, although one former student from the high school was with him when it happened. His dive buddy had been a big man on campus when he was in high school. In addition, he had been the quarterback for the football team last year.

The two were in sight of each other when the kid saw Jeff was in trouble. The report quoted him as saying he went to Jeff as quick as he could but was not able to help him. Gunny dropped a copy of the report off at my office one afternoon.

Since the day after Jeff's funeral, the mystery lady had called me on three occasions. I was convinced she was calling from a pay phone in the high school. What I originally thought was a party had to be kids in the background, and on two calls she had to leave when the eight thirty bell rang. Even though she would not give me her name she appeared to be a student who took getting to class on time as a serious matter.

I opened the office at eight, spread the paper out on my desk, and settled back to drink a cup of coffee I bought at the drive-through when the phone rang. It was her.

"Mister Maxwell?" she asked over the same noise I usually heard.

"Good morning." I didn't know exactly how to proceed with her, but I thought I might as well be nice. I even asked about the weather. We had virtually a one-way conversation for a minute with me doing most of the talking.

"Look, why don't we set up some kind of meeting. I think you trust me or you wouldn't keep calling." I sipped the hot coffee and waited for her to respond.

"I—I don't know. Where would we meet? I have to be home right after school." She hesitated. "Except on Thursdays. We usually have a Glee Club meeting then. Maybe I could skip..."

"No. Don't skip your meeting." I hesitated. "Do you come into town? I can meet you in my office." I had to admit she had me mildly curious about the nature of the calls. So far I knew only that she felt Jeff had been doing something in Portland that she felt was not exactly proper. And it might have had to do with his duty as a counselor for the school.

"I'll try to come by on Wednesday afternoon. We get out half a day for a teacher's meeting. Do you have a back door? I really don't want anybody to see me talking to you. I mean, if Nelson saw me—"

I heard the bell ring in the background. I knew she was about to hang up. "Come in through the parking lot. I'll leave the back door open." I tried one last shot. "Nelson who."

"I've got to go." She hung up and the line went dead.

I took the tape from the recorder on the phone, placed it in my desk machine, rewound it and listened to her voice again. It was a very soft quiet pleasant voice. A long time ago I once fell in love with a girl's voice over the phone. I was a year out of high school, facing an uncertain future, and had a double basic load of raging hormones. I spoke to this telephone beauty for two weeks before I had an evening off from my job at the auto parts store where I worked.

She was a student at a business college in town so we agreed to meet in the lobby of her dorm. We worked out a series of elaborate signals with her jingling her keys as she sat on a couch by the telephone in the lobby. I arrived a few minutes early, picked up a magazine, and waited for her to arrive.

And arrive she did! The elevator bringing her from the top floor had no choice but to be headed down. She stood a full six feet five inches. She was not overweight but she was big, with a capital B. I'd always been partial to a woman who would not beat me in an arm wrestling match if it came time to try. She was a pretty woman but she was intimidating. I did the only honorable thing possible at the time. I waited a few minutes as she jingled her keys, then I politely hauled ass. I'd never judged a person by their voice on the phone again.

By Wednesday afternoon, I had several conversations with George. All of them ended with his concern about the coach's death.

I slipped down to the Waterside Cafe for lunch and came straight back to my office to wait for my mystery visitor. I was reading the *Seattle PI* when I heard a noise at the back door.

I placed the paper on the desk and walked to the rear of my building. I wanted to see who the person was, but I sensed if I moved too quickly, she would escape like a frightened, wounded bird. Cautiously I opened the door.

The young women standing there was no more than seventeen. She had long dark hair and a mouth full of braces. Unlike many of the kids I saw around town before and after school, she did not dress like a reject from the Salvation Army Thrift Store. She wore a conservative, by local standards, skirt and blouse. Her singular fashion statement was a pair of upscale combat boots and a black beret of some soft material. Thirty years earlier, she would have been accused of trying for the Che Guevara look. Today I doubted if even her history teacher knew who Guevara was.

She was the first to speak.

"Mister Maxwell?" It was barely above a whisper, but it was the voice I had heard on the telephone.

I stepped back inside the door. "Please, come in. The office is empty."

She followed me without speaking.

I pulled a chair out for her and took a seat on the couch. I wanted to get away from behind my desk when we spoke. "If you drink coffee, I can pour you a cup. Otherwise, I've got some sodas in the back."

She looked around the office prior to answering. "A soda would be nice. Diet if you have it."

Fortunately, I started drinking diet soda a long time ago, so when I referred to them initially, I meant the diet kind.

"No problem, I'll get it." I stepped into the back room, retrieved the soda, poured it into a tall paper cup, and walked back to where she sat.

She sipped at the soda as she tried to get sufficient nerve to discuss why we were sitting there. Finally she spoke.

"I—I really shouldn't be here, you know. It's only because I know you and Coach Payton were friends and all. And—" She stopped in mid-sentence.

"And what?" I said, trying to get her to finish.

She stood as if to leave. "I really think I should be

going. I don't want anybody to see me here. They might—" She put her cup on the edge of my desk. She was quickly turning into that frightened bird who was about to fly. I felt I needed to stop her, or at least slow down her departure.

"Look, Coach Payton was a friend of mine. And my guess is he was a friend of yours, or you wouldn't have called me. If you just want to talk about him and his death to get it out of your head, I'm probably not the most qualified person you can find, but I'll listen. If there's more, nothing you say will leave this room.

I remembered my own daughters when a crisis entered their teenage lives. Sometimes they wanted to face it head-on, look the devil in the eye, and see who blinked first. Other times, they took the ostrich approach and buried their heads in the sand. Oftentimes, the hardest decision was which path to take. That battle was going on in front of me with my visitor.

She started to cry. "My grandfather died when I was nine. That's the only other person I know who's died. He lived in Texas, but I remember how he used to take my sister and me to the fair each year when he came to visit."

I had a box of tissues in my cabinet that I used to clean my glasses. I opened the door and handed her one. I was beginning to think she came here just to talk about Jeff and had nothing to add to the reasons for his death.

"I know I really loved my grandfather and it hurt when he died. A lot of people feel the same way about Jeff."

Not "Coach Payton. Or Mister Payton. Or Counselor Payton." But Jeff. I might be from the old school where kids were taught to call their teachers and people older than they were by their last names, but "Jeff" came too easy.

Across the street from my office, a man stopped by

the espresso stand, and I watched as he creamed, powdered, and sprinkled his way through a custom I was just now getting the hang of.

"I can't help you if I don't know what you want or what you want to talk about. I don't even know your name. Can we start with that?"

She stood and with a quick adjustment of her beret turned toward the back door. "I really think it's time for me to go. I shouldn't have bothered you."

My gut instinct told me there was more to this young mystery lady than a grieving student who needed to talk to a stranger. Kids were smarter today than in the past, so we were told. Read the papers and they told us they were faced with a myriad of problems unlike any generation in history. They faced drugs, guns, social problems, and diseases, which were enough to warp them just by thinking of the despair society had heaped upon them. The one thing they weren't given credit for was being kids. Way down deep inside, a seventeen-year-old girl was still a seventeen-year-old girl.

"Leave if you like. I'm sure Jeff would want you to trust me. He did." I hesitated as her steps slowed. "Especially about Portland."

She turned to face me. "You know about Portland?" Her little girl look quickly disappeared and so did she as she stepped through the still open doorway and into my parking lot.

# Chapter 5

Two days later I went back to the Edmonds Police Department. I called and made certain Gunny was there. I needed information and I didn't want to explain to too many people what I wanted or why. I knew Gunny would help all he could without asking too many questions.

He was in the squad room when I got there. "Mornin', Colonel. Need a cup of coffee?" Without waiting for a reply, he poured another mug and handed it to me. "I guess some old habits are too hard to break. I still can't get used to drinkin' all those fancy lattes and mochas. Far as I'm concerned, if it don't come out of a can, it ain't coffee." He waited a minute for a female employee to leave the room. "I don't guess you came over here because you can't afford to buy a cup of mud, huh."

"Not actually, Gunny. I'm still curious about—" Before I could finish, he did.

"The coach. I thought you'd be back. Has his wife hired you or is this on your own?"

I was immediately curious as to why Gunny might think Jeff's wife would hire me but I held back. "This is on my own. We'd been diving together a few times, and I knew how cautious he was. He just doesn't seem to be the kind who would die in a diving accident."

"That's why we have to tell electricians' wives their husband got electrocuted, and truck drivers die in road accidents, and roofers fall five stories. Hell, you know how it is. After a while, we all start to think we're bulletproof. You let your guard down for a second and, the next thing you know, somebody's shoveling dirt in your face and your wife's out buying a new car." He walked from the room and I followed. "You haven't seen Tracy at one of the car dealerships up on Aurora Avenue, have you?" he asked, over his shoulder.

We went into the squad room where Gunny picked up a clipboard with his daily orders on it. "Nothing like that, but she's human. And a damn good-looking one, at that. No kids. A good job. She'll be looking before long." He stopped and turned to face me. "Hell, she may be looking right now for all you know."

All my instincts said Gunny knew or suspected something he wasn't telling me. He was about to leave for his daily patrols so I had to ask quickly. "Has the autopsy report come back?"

Gunny hesitated then walked to a file cabinet. "I thought you wanted more than a cup of coffee, Colonel." He pulled the ancient gray cabinet open, ruffled through a few folders then extracted one. "We're supposed to be a paperless office. Everything's on computer. We tried that and most of us couldn't find our ass with both hands and a search warrant." He looked at the folder. "This'll tell you what you want to know. I'll make you a copy."

Later that day, I sat in my office reading the police report which was attached to the coroner's autopsy report. It was very simple. Drowning was the cause of death. According to the one witness, his diving partner, the two of them had made a routine dive in the Edmonds

Underwater Park. His dive buddy that day was Nelson Roberts. Nelson was now in the Community College. Nelson's statement said the dive was uncomplicated. They both owned their equipment, so they came prepared for the dive. They filled their tanks at the Dive Locker and went straight to the park. So far it was no different than the dives Jeff and I made together.

I was interrupted by a phone call from a local business owner who wanted to hire me to collect several bad checks one of his employees had taken. From the sound of it, there was more than a bad check involved. I agreed to meet him the first part of next week and went back to the report. Approximately twenty minutes into the dive, Jeff and Nelson were passing some of the old wrecks they had in the park. According to Nelson, he lost sight of Jeff for a few minutes. He saw him moving through the piles of cement and cables from the old dry dock that was also a part of the park. Nelson then stated the next thing he saw was that Jeff's tank was trapped in some metal from the old dock or by a piece of concrete that fell on him. By the time he was able to reach him, Jeff had panicked and drowned. I turned the page and found the coroner's report. There were injuries on Jeff, consistent with him having been caught in debris. He had numerous cuts and abrasions and his right wrist was severely bruised and broken. That's where Nelson said the block of cement fell.

It was all nice and neat, and my gut instinct said to not believe a word of it.

I was still sitting and holding the reports when the door opened and Leigh walked into the office.

I stood and walked over to help her with her coat. "Wow, you're up early today. Couldn't sleep or did you just miss me so bad you had to come down?"

"Don't flatter yourself. I came down here for two

reasons. I need to pay my cable bill before they cut it off. I thought I paid it last month and then I found the check in the glove box of the car, so I brought both of them down here today."

"Okay," I teased, "that's one reason. What's the second? You said there were two."

"Buy me lunch and I'll tell you." She looked back toward the street to see if anyone was nearby. When she saw it was clear, she leaned forward and gave me a kiss.

"You keep that up and I may have the landlord paint the windows black."

We walked up the street to one of the many trendy cafes in the city. This was a city where you could get a sandwich made from any number of things, as long as one of them wasn't red meat. For the basic hamburger with onions and greasy fries, you had to go up to one of the fast food places or the little hamburger stand near the high school. We decided to rough it and eat in town. Leigh had a healthy meal of some sort and I opted for a large bowl of soup and a spinach salad. We made small talk until the meal was served.

I reached into the basket of rolls, took one out, buttered it for her and placed it on her bread plate. "Okay, what's the second reason you came to town?"

"To get you to pay for lunch, what else?" When she smiled her eyes picked up any available light, magnified it a thousand times, and it danced between us. Sometimes, it was all I could do to keep from taking her in my arms each time we were together. I was on the edge of being crazy about her, and she knew it, but between us we had enough excess baggage to fill a rail car. A lot of it had to go, or there would never be a little cottage with a single last name on the front door.

We finished lunch and walked back to my office. On the way we stopped in a shop specializing in things made from pieces of driftwood, and designs painted on rocks. Leigh bought a series of three smooth stones with waterfront scenes painted on them. When she took them to the counter to pay, I stood beside her.

"I—I saw both of you at Coach Payton's funeral—didn't I?" The young girl behind the counter was obviously a student at the High School.

"We were there," I said. "Did you have Mister Payton for any classes?"

"No. He mostly worked with the senior girls. I'll be a senior next year. I did like him, though. He was real nice to all of us."

"I know. He was a friend of mine too."

Leigh paid and we left.

When we got back to my office, I had one phone message. It was from a company wanting me to switch my phone service. I often wondered how much tele marketers made. They seemed to be one of the most dedicated and growing segments of the work force. I got three or four calls a week from somebody wanting to sell me something. Unfortunately, if they were working on commission, those who called me were probably on the poverty rolls.

"I've got to be going. Will I see you tonight?" Leigh stood framed in the doorway, the sunlight to her back. The lady definitely displayed well.

"I'll pick you up when you get off. I may come by earlier and have dinner. I'm getting tired of pasta and frozen desserts."

She left and the quiet of the office was overwhelming. I reached behind my desk and turned on the radio. I had it set to an "oldies" station, so I was not surprised when Frank Sinatra's voice filled the quiet with his version of "Night and Day."

I sat listening for a moment, then I went back to the

reports I picked up from Gunny. During the time I spent in the Military Police Corps in the army, I was in charge of many investigations of death under unusual or suspicious conditions. Several had turned out to be homicides. Others were suicides. But the vast majority were simply deaths under unusual or suspicious circumstances. Nothing more, nothing less. Generally they were undistinguishable on the surface. It was a lead from a party involved, or some hard evidence, that caused us to reopen the case or look at the circumstances in a different manner. We didn't do it on gut instincts. There was a little thing called probable cause. That gave the investigators the reason they needed to pursue the investigation and make an arrest if it was warranted. It worked the same in the civilian world.

By the time Frank finished his song, I came to the realization that all the rationale I had used on myself didn't matter. I wasn't in the army, and I wasn't on the Edmonds Police Force. I didn't have to play by any of those rules. I could make up my own rules as I went along. If I wanted to follow my gut, I could. I picked up the phone and punched in a number.

The phone was answered on the second ring. "The Dive Locker. May I help you?"

I recognized the voice as that of Ralph Stewart. He and two other men owned the shop, however, only Ralph worked there. The others were silent partners.

"Ralph, its Max. I want to dive the Underwater Park, but I don't have a partner. You got anyone down there looking for a dive this afternoon?"

"Hang on, Max. I'll see." He put the phone on hold and I was treated to several minutes of a Caribbean steel band playing calypso versions of songs I recognized but couldn't identify. I found myself beginning to enjoy the music when Ralph came back.

"Got a lady down here looking at a new regulator. She did a check dive with us last month. Seems to be all right. I'll let you talk to her." Before I could say anything, there was a pause and then a female voice came on the line.

"Hi, this is Anna. With whom am I speaking?"

I introduced myself over the phone, told her what I wanted to do, and invited her to join me. I told her Ralph would vouch for me, and I even invited her for a cup of coffee prior to the dive if she had any hesitations or suspicions. She surprised me by agreeing to make the dive that afternoon. Anna said she needed an hour to go home and get her gear. We agreed to meet at the dive shop at three thirty.

I went to my place and got my gear. My tanks were almost empty from my last dive. When I got to the Dive Locker, it was a little early so I filled the two canisters. I was looking at some photographs Ralph had of the Underwater Park when the door opened and I heard Ralph greet the person as Anna.

The first thing I noticed about my new dive buddy was that she had class. It was class that comes with the birth certificate. Anna was about five seven, blonde hair, and skin the color of toast. No fake 'n bake for this lady. Her tan was either natural or obtained on beaches surrounded by palm trees and drinks with little umbrellas in them. When Ralph pointed toward me, she glided rather than walked to me.

"I'm Anna. Mister Stewart said you're Mister Maxwell." She held out her hand.

"If we're going to dive together I think we should be on a first name basis, Anna. Everyone calls me Max." I took her hand. "I hope this wasn't too short of a notice for you."

"No problem. I've wanted to dive the park since I did

my check dive. This is a good excuse not to stall any longer. And if we're going to use first names I pronounce mine Anna as in Madonna, not Anna as in Banana. Her eyes glanced down. I was still holding her hand. I quickly dropped it and tried to make up for the social error and my blushing by talking much too fast.

"I filled my tanks when I first got here. Do you need to fill up?"

Anna smiled and shook her head. She had diamond stud earrings that probably measured three-quarter carat in each ear.

We loaded our gear after changing into our dry suits. My suit was a black one I had been using for years. Hers was probably from a dive boutique in the Caribbean. It was a rainbow of colors, all of which looked perfectly natural on her.

When we got to the park, I unloaded all the gear. Anna carefully checked her tanks, regulator, hoses, and BC. Before she could slip them on, I came to her and placed a map of the park out on the tail gate of my Toyota.

I traced the route on the map as I spoke. "If you don't mind, here's where I'd like to go once we get into the park." I pointed to a spot I had circled on the map.

"This is your dance. You lead, I'll follow." Her voice had a slight accent to it. It didn't sound foreign, but I was certain she was not a native of the Pacific Northwest.

We put on our gear and slipped slowly into the cold water of that portion of Puget Sound known as Brackett's Landing. No matter what time of year you went diving in the Sound, it was cold. It still took a minute for the body to get accustomed to the change in temperature as one enters the water. We used our snorkels for a few yards, then I began to tread water as Anna pulled up beside me.

"You okay?" I asked when she swam beside me.

"Never better."

"Let's do it!" I pulled my mask down and motioned for her to dive.

The water was only slightly murky with a visibility of about fifteen to twenty feet. I had my light and a map, so I knew where we were going. I swam around the wrecks for a while, pointing out some of the interesting sights to Anna. Each time I did so, she flashed me a quick thumbs up signal in approval. I made my way over to the old dry dock and to the point I had circled on my map.

Large chunks of concrete from the old dock lay strewn about the floor of the park. Many were still connected to the dock with umbilical cords of steel re-enforcing rods. Several large chunks were balanced precariously on each other.

This was where Jeff had died. I did a mental replay of how I thought it happened. He swam between two large chunks and some of the protruding rebar. His tanks hit one of the large chunks. It slipped from its perch of thirty years and, at that precise moment in time, it fell. He was trapped. He struggled to get free and in his panic he lost his mouthpiece. By the time he or his young, and probably near-panicked dive-partner, realized what was going on, he had sucked in too much of the Puget Sound to survive.

I was staring at the spot when I was startled by Anna tapping me on the shoulder. I used my flippers to turn in the water to face her. She held her hand out in a motion that was unmistakable. "Is everything all right?"

It was my time to give her the thumbs up in response.

We swam cautiously through the rubble for another twenty minutes. After I had seen all I wanted to for that dive, I got Anna's attention, tapped my watch, and indicated we should surface.

She nodded in agreement, and we slowly made our way to the surface.

Anna pulled her regulator from her mouth and reached beside her mask for her snorkel. It had slipped around during the dive, and she was unable to reach it. I swam to her and slid it around her mask until it was in a position where she could use it. I watched as she slipped gracefully forward in the water and, with her face down, swam to the shore.

I hated snorkels. It was one of those great mysteries of life for me. Everyone I knew, and went diving with, could put the long tube in their mouth, lay face forward in the water, and swim for days. I tried the same thing, and I lowered the water level of the Sound or the ocean by at least a foot as I drank and choked my way to shore. That day was no exception. By the time I reached the small area known to the locals as the beach, I had consumed at least ten times the recommended daily allowance of Brackett's Landing.

On the shore, Anna peeled her hood off and shook out her shoulder length blonde hair. As she ran her hands through it, I noticed she was still wearing her diamond studs. Either they were some of the best fakes I had ever seen, or my initial evaluation was correct. She had class and money and took both for granted.

"That was great. I've wanted to dive the Underwater Park for several weeks." She bent to pick up the tanks she had slipped from her back when she got to the beach. It was impossible not to look when she bent at the waist. Her movement was smooth and graceful. I guessed dance or aerobics took up some of her free time.

"If you'll carry the small stuff, I'll take the tanks." I placed my flippers, mask, and snorkel in my dive bag. Without waiting for a reply, I took the tanks from her and started toward the Toyota.

She picked up the bag and walked beside me. "Isn't this where the gentleman from the school drowned last week?"

"Yeah. Unfortunately, we lose a few people out here every year. Most of them are inexperienced divers who think they can come from three dives in Cancun or Hawaii and hit the cold water here without getting a check dive first."

"Is that what happened to him?"

We were at the Toyota. I opened the back door and we placed our gear inside.

"No, Jeff's was an accident of some sort. They say a piece of cement fell on him. He was trapped, and he panicked, trying to get loose. By the time he realized he was in trouble, it was too late to correct the error. He was low on air. He got into trouble, panicked and drowned. It happens to the most experienced divers." I had all the gear packed inside. I walked around to the passenger's side and opened the door for Anna.

I had placed large towels on the seats for us before we hit the water. Anna sat on one and used the other to wrap around her shoulders. She surprised me as I backed from my parking place.

"I take it you don't believe your friend drowned. Or perhaps it was not as accidental as reported." She turned in the seat to face me. "The two of you were far too good for something like that to just happen."

"I'm sorry. Just how much do you k—know about m—me?" I stammered.

"I don't risk my life with just anyone, Mister Maxwell. I did a quick check on you prior to our dive. Are you working for someone, or are you just doing this because Mister Payton was a friend?"

I drove slowly down the road between the water and the railroad tracks. "This is for me. Jeff and I made a few dives together. He was an excellent diver. He had just completed certification on his instructor card so he could teach some of the kids at the school. It just doesn't add up. Or at least, not to me."

"Did we dive the area where he drowned?"

I nodded in silence.

"I thought so. It was where I startled you, wasn't it?" I felt her hand on my arm as she spoke.

The Dive Locker was only a few minutes' drive from the spot where we entered the water. I pulled into the shop's parking lot without responding.

"Which car is yours?"

"Over there, the Lexus."

I slipped into a vacant spot beside her car. Unlike mine, which always seemed to need washing, her car was spotless. From a small bag she had left in my Toyota, she removed a remote door key system. I barely heard the sound as she activated it and the driver's door and the trunk lid opened.

She stepped into the parking lot and reached into her trunk for a small gym bag. "If you'll put my stuff in the trunk, I'll go inside and change. I'd hate to drive home in a rubber suit." She hesitated and then held out her hand. "I really enjoyed the dive. Perhaps we can do it again." She reached inside her bag and pulled out an old fashioned silver cigarette case. She flipped the top to open it. When she did so, it was filled with her personal cards. She extracted one and handed it to me.

"Give me a call—and a little more notice if possible." She turned and walked into the shop.

By the time I got inside, she was already in the changing room.

Ralph saw me come in. He was opening a box filled with face masks. "How'd it go? Did you guys have a good dive?"

"Good. Good dive. She's obviously got plenty of tank time under her belt."

"I didn't think she'd disappoint you."

I was headed toward the men's changing room when she reemerged without her dry suit. She had changed into a pair of jeans and a white shirt. The clothes and a quick application of make-up and she was a new woman. She smiled and waved at both of us when she left.

This time of year it got dark in the Puget Sound between six thirty and seven. I got back to the office just as the last rays of the sun slipped peacefully across the western peninsula. The sunset in the Pacific Northwest became a gift from us to Hawaii each day after we were through enjoying it.

When I arrived at my office, my intention was to check my mail and messages and finalize the appointment I had the next week at the shopping mall. That idea went down the tubes the minute I pushed the red button and listened to the messages on my phone machine.

The first message was a female voice I had never heard before. She left a number and said I should call the minute I returned. I wrote the number on the back of an envelope on my desk and pushed the button for the second of five blinks.

Number two was the man I was to meet at the mall next week. I already had his number, so there was nothing to write from this one. It was the third message that threw everything into a tailspin. It was the same voice as number one, but this time she left more than a number.

"Mister Maxwell, I need to speak to you. I know you were a friend of Jeff Payton's and you're looking into his death. I believe I know who did it and why." The voice began to soften. "It—It was my husband. Please call me."

I couldn't grab the handset quickly enough to dial her number.

# Chapter 6

I spent the next two hours trying to reach the woman on the phone. Each time I called, I got a recording. It was a friendly enough recording, telling me I'd reached the number and I could leave a message for either Barry or Marge. Since she had called me and, considering the message she left, I did not leave one in return.

At eight, I left the office and walked up the street to the library. I got a copy of the telephone cross directory in order to look up the street address using the phone number. It was a handy little trick used by real estate agents, tele marketers, burglars, and private investigators. If you knew the phone number, you could sometimes find out the street address. *Sometimes* was the operative word. If the phone was unlisted it would not be in the directory. Such was the case with Barry and Marge. Their number was conveniently missing from the directory.

If I didn't hear from her soon, I planned to call an old friend at the phone company and use a trick that was even older than the cross directory. A well-placed bribe usually worked with great efficiency.

I walked back to my office. It was now almost nine. Edmonds was not a hotbed of activity during the day and, with the exception of the local theater playing second-run features, there was little activity on the streets past seven in the evening.

Old habits die hard so, when I neared my office, I slowed my pace and looked around the streets. There was only one car parked in my block. It was up the street and across from my place. I could see a woman sitting behind the wheel on the driver's side. My gut told me it was Marge.

I opened my door and turned on a light. Normally, I would have kept the lights low, picked up my brief case, and left. If my guess was right, I wanted the lady on the street to feel comfortable. I was almost to my desk when the phone rang.

"Maxwell here." I could tell from the static it was a cellular call. My guess was it came from across the street. There was a long hesitation and I answered for the second time.

"Mister Maxwell—I—called earlier." It was the same voice.

"I'm here. You can talk to me on the phone or you can come down." I took a chance and continued. "I'm down the street on the right. You can park in front on the street or use the alley and park out back."

There was a moment's hesitation and then the line went dead.

I went to the front of my place and looked up the street. The car was already moving. It was driving with no headlights and, as it neared the alleyway between my building and one of the many taverns that dotted the city, it slowed and turned. I went to the back door and opened it. There was sufficient light spilling into the parking lot from the slightly open doorway, so that my visitor could tell the door was available to her. I went to my desk and waited.

I heard the door scrape along the floor as it was opened wider by my visitor. Another old habit that was hard to rid myself of was to always be prepared. I had a concealed weapons permit but I rarely found myself in a position to carry it. I did, however, have a pistol I kept in my desk drawer. The sound of me opening my drawer was muffled by the person walking through my back room. I kept my ungentlemanly posture and remained sitting when the woman came into view.

"I'm Maxwell. And you are…" I asked as she came in.

"I think I'd rather not say, just yet." She was not nearly as nervous in person as on the phone. She looked around the office and indicated a chair near the wall and away from the window and the lamp. "May I sit here?"

I nodded as she took her seat.

"Just how well did you know Jeff Payton?" She pulled a pack of cigarettes from her purse and offered me one. "Do you smoke?"

"No thanks, I quit some time ago. But I don't mind if you—"

Before I could finish, she put the pack back in her purse. "That's all right. I've found if I ask if I can smoke, most people are too polite to tell me not to. If I offer them a cigarette and they refuse, then I don't smoke." She stared at the pack for a moment before speaking again. "You didn't answer me. How well did you know Jeff?"

"I knew him professionally from the school. He had been the counselor for one of my daughters a few years ago and I saw a couple of football games when he took the team to the state championship. On the personal side, he and I went diving several times. But this is not about me." I hesitated. "How about you, Marge? How well did you know Jeff?"

She laughed slightly. "You called my house, didn't

you? We have a machine that counts the number of hang-up we get on the phone. We also have caller ID. The number was blocked on the first one of the hang-ups. I figured it must have been you."

I had caller blocking placed on my phone at the office and at home as soon as it was available. In my line of business, it was sometimes wise not to let people know you were trying to reach them.

"How well did I know Jeff?" She repeated my question then she closed her eyes and tilted her head back slightly. "As well as anyone, including his wife, could know him. But then I guess I'm not the only woman who can make that claim." She hesitated as she drifted away to that secret place women went to when they think. "I would guess that you don't know nearly enough about Jeff to be doing what you're doing."

"Do you wanna fill in some blank spots I need to know about?" I stood and went to the coffee maker, and switched it on. "I'll make a pot. It'll be ready in about four minutes. And then you can tell me more." I walked to the back room and got two mugs, a small container of sugar, chemical sweeteners in several different colors, and a handful of creamers I picked up at the bakery when I got a cup to go. By the time I got back to my office area, the coffee was running dark and almost drinkable. We both were quiet while I watched the stream of coffee decrease until it stopped. I pulled the filter portion from the machine and sat it on the back sink. I poured two mugs and handed her one. "Would you like anything in it?" I slid the creamers and sweeteners over to her side of the table where I had the pot.

"You must not be a native of Seattle. It's hard to find a plain cup of coffee up here," she said over the rim of her mug.

"Transplanted years ago, but I've got too many gallons of army coffee in my system to change now." The conversation died at that point. I waited for her to speak.

"Why are you interested in Jeff's death? Is someone paying you to look into it? Don't you usually have to hire a private investigator to get them to work for you?" She took a long pull from the mug. "At least that's how they do it on television and in the movies."

"The real world is a little different. Sometimes I do things simply because I want to or because they need doing."

"So you've not been hired by someone."

"I didn't say that."

"But you said—"

"Look, on the phone you said you knew who killed Jeff and why they did it. What makes you think it wasn't an accident?"

"You don't think it was an accident. If you did, you wouldn't be looking into it like you're doing."

"I think you're playing a game, Marge. If you have some information on his death, why don't you go to the police? They can reopen the case. If your information is valid, they'll bring the person responsible to justice. Isn't that what you want? If it wasn't an accident, you do want the person responsible punished, don't you?"

"I'm not certain."

I sat on the edge of my desk facing her. "About what? If it was an accident or if the person responsible should be punished?"

"If the person I think is responsible did it, then I know it wasn't an accident."

"Bottom line, Marge, you think your husband is responsible for Jeff's death?" I leaned forward. I didn't want to miss it if she confirmed it was her husband.

Marge sat her mug on the table and ran her finger around the rim of the heavy container. She got up and walked to the window overlooking Main Street in Edmonds, Washington. Outside two people were leaving a restaurant across the street. Other than that, the streets were empty. The clock on my radio behind my desk was blinking nine fifty-one.

At nine minutes to ten in the evening, Marge turned to face me. "My husband killed Jeff Payton."

# Chapter 7

It was almost time for Leigh to get off when I got to Hart's. I had spent the previous hour with Marge, talking about more things than I thought possible. She had convinced herself when she heard about Jeff's death that her husband Barry had all the components for doing him in. She explained that he had opportunity and the knowledge of how to do it. What she didn't discuss in detail was motive. And although she was convinced, I wasn't.

I parked in the nearly vacant lot and walked up the steps to the second floor restaurant. Hart's was a local chain. They had several other locations in the area. All were located on the water overlooking the Puget Sound. They had one in Edmonds, one on Lake Union in Seattle, and another overlooking the ferry in Mukilteo. They were just what I needed, on my budget and my palate. Mid-range in price and food on the menu I recognize and could pronounce.

Leigh had been the hostess there for just a week or two when I met her. There was an immediate attraction on both our parts, although she was not too quick to admit it. The first night I saw her, she was still in a training mode. The former hostess was taking over some administrative position at the corporate headquarters but was hanging around long enough to show Leigh whom to sit where, when a local high-roller came in with no reservations. I never knew when I would eat there so I never made reservations. A bar table was usually where I had dinner. That night was a mid-week evening, so there were a few empty tables in the main dining room when a smiling and friendly Leigh greeted me. I let her seat me next to the window overlooking the ferry making its way to Kingston. I think we even exchanged a few comments on the walk back to the table. I noticed two more tables filled and then a local businessman came in.

I had seen the guy around town. He was one of the men who had been in town since Edmonds actually was a town and not an expensive and trendy bedroom community for Seattle. At one time, his business may actually have been profitable and thriving. In those days he could go to any place in town and immediately be shown to his favorite table. Unfortunately for him, his favorite table at Hart's was occupied that particular evening. I was the occupant.

I could hear Leigh trying to explain to him that they held reservations for fifteen minutes, and then let the tables go. He was now over thirty minutes late. Since I had only ordered a drink, under normal conditions, I would have gone to the hostess, told her I overheard the conversation, and offered to move. I would have done it that night, but this guy suddenly became an asshole about the situation.

Even with his wife trying to calm him, he was getting much too loud and almost threatening. The bartender and I arrived at about the same time at the desk where Leigh was holding her own with the man.

He turned to me when he recognized me as the person occupying his table.

"I want you off my table before I—"

He never got to finish his sentence because he made the mistake of attempting to use his forefinger in my chest to punctuate his displeasure with the situation. It was a quick and simple takedown. I really did not break his finger on purpose.

Naturally there was a threat to call the police and the promise of a lawsuit against Hart's and me. He was escorted from the place by the bartender and a cook who had done hard time at the state pen in Monroe. I got my dinner free and, by the time the dust settled and all the paperwork was completed, I had a date with Leigh. Since then, both Leigh and I had become fixtures at Hart's. Leigh was totaling up whatever she totaled at the end of the night when I got to the top of the stairs. She saw me and smiled.

No matter how many times I saw it or what kind of mood I was in, her smile had a soothing effect on me.

She looked up from her counting without losing her place. "This won't take long tonight. If you want to wait in the bar, I'll be through in a few minutes."

I sat in one of the seats used by those people waiting for their tables. "I think I'll wait out here tonight."

She looked up at me again. "Are you all right? Do you have another migraine?"

"No. No migraine. I'm fine. I just want to take in your ravishing beauty tonight."

She smiled as I talked and returned to her work with a last look at me that said she wasn't certain if I was joking, drunk, serious, or what.

It was almost one a.m. when we left. I steered Leigh to her car, and she gave me the keys without discussion.

It was a beautiful night. The sky was a deep blue that could pass for black anywhere in the world. The stars danced overhead like a million kids with sparklers had been turned loose to play. I got on the main street out of town and headed toward I-5 and Seattle.

Leigh settled in the seat and turned sideways to face me. "You want to talk about it?"

Sometimes, I thought she could actually read my mind. It was a scary thought, considering some of the things that rambled around in there unchecked on occasion. "I had a visitor today. It was a friend of Jeff Payton's. She seemed to think his death may not have been an accident and her husband may have been involved."

I kept Leigh's Miata at the speed limit as we made our way South. At the intersection for the express lane, the state patrol had a car pulled to the side.

The driver was trying to touch his nose without falling on his ass. There was little doubt he would be a guest of the city for the night.

"I'm not certain what to think. I did a dive at the Underwater Park this afternoon. I saw the approximate area where he drowned. It could have happened."

"But…"

"Yeah, but. I've only known two other divers who got into trouble and panicked enough to drown. And one of them may have actually had a heart attack."

"You didn't dive by yourself, did you?"

I hesitated before I answered. "No, I called Stewart at the Dive Locker and he found somebody to dive as my partner." I glanced at Leigh to see if she knew instinctively my partner was a very attractive woman.

We crossed the Ship Canal Bridge, and I slid the car to the right lane. "Are you in the mood for a little decadence and debauchery?"

"Not the whips and chains again?"

I pulled off the interstate and made our way to the fringe of Lake Union. "Not tonight. This time, it's the whipped cream, anchovies, and peanuts."

Leigh ruffled her hair in the night air circulating through the car. "Good. Nothing too kinky."

We passed several restaurants and clubs on the way to our destination. Lake Union was one of the two large lakes formed by the Puget Sound in Seattle. The other was Lake Washington. Both had become a Mecca for upscale living, with Lake Washington hosting the house of America's richest man and Seattle's favorite son, Bill Gates. Our destination was one that we often came to after a particularly difficult day.

Nestled between two restaurants on Lake Union was a place with seven open-air hot tubs. Each large old California redwood tub was seated on a cement slab, and the whole set-up was enclosed from its neighbor by a thin, but completely private three-sided privacy fence. The open end of the tub enclosure faced Lake Union and each had an unobstructed view. Overhead, part of the tub area was a canopy that kept out some of the rain but none of the stars on nights such as this. When you checked in, you were given towels and a warm robe. In each tub area was yet another warmer so if you were inclined to get out of the tub you could wrap yourself in the warmth of the robe.

Leigh and I quickly changed from our street clothes to the robes and proceeded to our tub. We walked down the hallway leading from the locker rooms just off the lobby to the outdoor area where the tubs were snuggled against a slight hillside. Once we were in the confines of our tub area, I couldn't help but admire Leigh as she slowly let the robe slide to the ground and stepped into the steamy tub. She turned to face me and slipped beneath the water till it lapped at her nipples. I was more than ready to join her.

For the next hour we forgot about her work and mine. There was no outside world. Everything we wanted was enveloped in the warm cloud rising from the tub. She lay with her head resting against the edge of the tub and let her body float on the warm surface. The first time we visited the place, she was concerned that someone on a passing boat could see us. This time it did not matter as she came to me and we made love in the mist.

An hour later, we once again pulled onto I-5, and I pointed the Miata toward Edmonds. She was asleep before we got out of the parking lot. She left me alone with my thoughts of things that had happened during the day. In my mind, Jeff's death now was firmly planted in the category of suspicious, very suspicious. If what Marge had told me in my office was true, there might have been several people with plenty of reason to be extremely pissed at him. I wanted to know if that anger was enough to actually cause them to kill him. As we passed the King County sign, I knew the best way to find out was to do something I'd probably regret. I was going to pay a visit to Tracy Payton, Jeff's widow.

I spent the night at Leigh's after stopping by Hart's to pick up my Toyota. I had a hell of a time waking Leigh up sufficiently so she could drive her car back to her place. At one point, while stopped at a red light, I thought I saw her head drop in a quick doze. I promised myself we would not visit the hot tubs again if she had to drive afterward. They were just too relaxing.

I'd gotten to the point where I almost hated weekends. I seemed to spend most of the time looking for something to do. When I had a family, there was always yard work or repairs to the house or something involving the kids. All of that was gone now.

On Saturday morning, I sometimes went to my office and, if I had nothing else to do, I spent the time reading the paper. I used every excuse not to stay in my apartment. Leigh usually had to work, so if we did anything, it was during the afternoon when she awakened.

Sunday evening at Leigh's place turned into Sunday night. I didn't go home. Leigh was still sleeping the next morning when I slipped from beside her, grabbed a shower, dressed, and left. I took the long way to the office and stopped by the Treetopper for breakfast. They had a special on Mondays. When you entered, there was a sign announcing that their coffee pot had been cleaned over the weekend and the coffee was fresh. Anytime I waited more than a week between visits, I had to get to know a whole new crew of workers, with the exception of Claude the cook and owner and his wife or girlfriend Sue. They had been married and divorced from each other at least three times since I'd known them. She seemed to always keep his last name, so it took a scorecard to know what their marital status happened to be at any one time.

Sue brought me a large brown mug of coffee. She never carried a pad with her. If she took the order from a table of twenty-five, she would have memorized the whole thing in one try. "Same as always?" she asked as the mug slid across the table.

The first time I came in, I ordered a ham, cheese, and jalapeno omelet with hash browns, toast, and coffee. I never got a chance to change it. From then on, every time I came in, her question never changed, and neither did my breakfast.

I finished my breakfast, had another cup of coffee, and left. On the way out, I stopped at one of the last pay phones in the city and dialed the number I had for Jeff when I called him at home. After three rings, Tracy answered.

"Tracy? Hi. It's Max. Is this too early for you?" I knew she was spending some time at home prior to going back to teaching. I hoped I hadn't awakened her.

"No, it's fine. What can I do for you, Max?"

That was the hard part. How did you tell a grieving widow you thought her husband might not have died as she thought? Even worse, I still had the bomb Marge dropped on me the previous evening. "Can I see you sometime today? Perhaps I can buy you lunch." I wanted to test the waters with her before I told her anything. If lunch went without a problem, I would try to get her back to the office or her place for the privacy we needed.

"Yes, I think I'd like that. I really need to get out."

"Great. I'll pick you up at twelve-thirty. Is that okay?" That would give me time to see my other client at his business and find out how much he was missing from his till.

"Twelve-thirty. Fine, I'll look forward to it." She stopped talking but she didn't break the connection. "Max? Is everything all right?"

"Oh, yeah. No real problems. I just wanted to talk to you a bit." I hated doing business over the phone.

I left the Treetopper and hit Aurora Avenue North. Every city I'd ever lived in had its equivalent of Aurora. It was the street where you could get everything up to, and including, a case of leprosy on the street corner. Numerous legitimate businesses were surrounded by used car lots, trailer parks, sleazy motels—either rented to hookers by the hour or to construction workers by the month—and enough adult entertainment to satisfy even the most perverse appetites. It was mid-town America's version of the old Forty-Second and Broadway, the Deuce, in New York.

I found a parking place at the regional mall, just outside the city limits, and went inside. Once in the mall, I went straight to the small gift shop where I was to meet the owner. I recognized him the minute I entered. He was trying to be everywhere and everything at once. There were two other people working as clerks, but it was his show all the way. I watched him politely ask one woman if he could help her. When she didn't answer quickly enough, he turned his attention to another person standing nearby. By the time the first lady decided, there was no one to assist her. This didn't strike me as the way to run a successful retail business. I waited until I could get his attention.

"Mister Tice, I'm Maxwell. We have an appointment." I handed him my card. If he was experiencing employee theft, I did not want to be known by the people working for him. "I think we should talk outside the shop. Can you leave for a few minutes?"

He held the card for a moment before it registered who I was and why he wanted me there. "Oh, certainly. I'm sorry. I'd forgotten all about our meeting." He went toward the front counter. "Let me tell Debbie I'll be out for a few minutes." While he conferred with the young lady he called Debbie, I took a quick look around the shop.

It was filled with glassware, gifts, and things that had an instant appeal to a certain portion of the population. Fortunately, I could control myself. The shelves were filled with collector editions of paperweights and gnomes. Statues of little children in a variety of play modes were in glass-enclosed shelves next to models of houses from England. The stuff wasn't inexpensive.

I was looking at a plate with a scene from *Gone with the Wind* when he came up to the case. "That's a limited edition. One of our most popular sellers. Anything from *Gone with the Wind* is hot. They made a quarter million of that one then broke the mold." He looked at the plate almost like a kid looking at a Mantle rookie card.

"It's really nice but I don't think it would go with my silverware pattern."

The look he gave me was one of horror. For a fleeting second he was certain he had hired a man to protect his business and that man was ready to eat beans and franks from a *Gone with the Wind* plate. He finally cracked a half smile and led me from the shop.

We stopped at the food court and found a table in the far corner near the door leading to the parking lot.

"I've got three other businesses just like this one, Mister Maxwell. This is the busiest, so I spend more time here than at the others. When I'm not in the store, I know things are stolen. I want you to find out if it's customers or employees."

He provided me some of the initial information I needed, and he promised to stop by my office with a completed sheet which I gave him for each of his employees. Although some of the information may have been considered privileged, it was essential that I know if anyone had a police record or had been terminated from any other job for stealing. I suspected it was a combination of the business growing too big, too fast; his not keeping up with the books; and the type of employee thefts that simply came with the turf.

We talked a while and I watched him as he walked back to his shop. He gave me his card. On the back, he had penciled his home phone and the number for his cellular. Some of the biggest dollar losses to businesses were from unauthorized people having access to the owner's cellular phone number. Perhaps my initial instincts were correct. I let him get around the corner from the wing of the mall where we had met before I stood and walked to the exit. Late morning traffic was light, so I made it to Jeff's house five minutes early. Even though we had not been close friends, I still thought of him in the present, as if he was still with us. I guessed that was a defense mechanism against admitting someone was really dead. I remembered reading a story about a movie star's mother who said she never mentioned the star's father in the house after the parents divorced. The kid grew up never having her father's name spoken. When anyone asked why, the mother replied to the effect that, if she never mentioned him, the little girl might not realize he was missing. That was stretching it, but what the hell? If it worked…

I circled the block once to kill a minute or two and pulled up in front of what was once Jeff and Tracy's house. Now it was just Tracy's. It was not very old and had been built during the boom times in the nineties. It had more than doubled in value since real estate north of Seattle was almost as desirable as that across Lake Washington to the east.

I walked up the slight incline from the street to the house. It was just enough to give it an occasional view of the Puget Sound and the mountains on the peninsula. Tracy answered the door after I rang the bell.

"Max, won't you come in? I was just putting up the vacuum." She stepped aside for me to enter. "Actually, it was just the vacuum hoses. Jeff put in a central system for us last year. We're also—" She stopped and turned to face me with a half smile on her face. "I guess it'll take a while to stop referring to 'us' and 'we.'"

She turned away. I made no attempt to say or do anything. Finally she regained her composure and turned back to me. "So, you want to buy me lunch? I think that will be nice." Without waiting for a response from me, she re-opened the front door and we walked out.

Once in the Toyota, I headed toward Aurora Avenue. Along with everything else, the street had one of the best Mexican restaurants in the area. So many people called it El Sleazo, I was surprised the owner hadn't changed the name. From the outside, it looked like it had recently been the scene of a major battle between two warring factions. Inside, the food made up for any architectural shortcomings.

We got a table near the front. Both Tracy and I saw someone we knew and were visited by them. The word of Jeff's death had spread, and they stopped by the table long enough to pay their respects to her. A young Hispanic girl put a basket of warm chips and some high-octane salsa between us. I reached for the chips first.

"You can order anything you like. I think I'll stick with these. After a few of them my tongue is usually so desensitized, I can't taste anything, so why bother?" I dipped another chip and slowly raised it to my mouth.

"I think those are best when you've got a pitcher of marguerites. Jeff and I —" She stopped for a second "I'm afraid I may not be very good company today."

The waitress came back, and Tracy selected a lunch special. I decided to join her and ordered a number three. It was too early for me to start drinking but I offered to watch while she did.

"I think that may just put me over the edge right now. I better take a rain check and save it for later." For the first time, she smiled.

Our lunch came and we ate while making small talk. We both tap danced around any reference to Jeff. Finally, when we were through, I had to broach the subject of why I had asked Tracy to have lunch with me.

I paid the tab and, while the waitress went to get my change, I finally told Tracy about why I had asked her to lunch. "I've had several calls since the accident."

"Calls? What kind of calls?"

"Phone calls mostly but one came in person. All of them seem to think there may be more to Jeff's death than we know." I spoke carefully, not wanting to make more of it than I already had.

Tracy stared at me intently. "I don't think I understand. What do you mean when you say more?"

"I'm not really certain, but I think you and I should talk. Perhaps at my office. Someplace where we won't be disturbed."

The waitress brought my change. I took all but a couple of dollars that I left for her and slid my chair back from the table. I thought if I made the move, Tracy would follow. She did.

It took us less than ten minutes to get back to my parking place beside the building where my office was located. Occasionally someone would pull into my space when I left and the street side parking was filled. But today, it was still empty so I pulled in and walked around to open Tracy's door.

"Do you do that for everybody, or am I someone special?"

"Yes. On both counts. I guess growing up in the South never leaves you. I can't help it. I still open doors for a lady, and occasionally I find myself calling someone darlin'." She slid easily from the seat and we walked to the front of my building. When we approached the door, I noticed her drop back a step as I reached to open it for her.

Once inside, I offered her a seat on the couch. She took it and I sat across from her.

"You're not very good at this, you know," she said as I sat down. "I can't imagine you trying to tell a woman it was over between the two of you or something equally distasteful. It would take you two weeks. Why don't you tell me what's on your mind? I think I can handle almost anything right now."

"I guess I have been kinda obvious, haven't I?" I took a good look at Tracy and wondered how she would react to the speculation I was about to share with her. "At the restaurant, I said I've had a couple of calls about the accident. At least two of the callers didn't want to let Jeff's death be officially classified as an accident."

"Not an accident? Then what? Do you think Jeff was the kind of man to commit suicide?" As soon as she said the word, she knew I wasn't talking about suicide. "Oh, my God! Do you mean you think he was—was murdered?"

# Chapter 8

I remembered one incident that happened when I was in the army. I was a captain stationed at Fort Benning, Georgia. It was a time in the army when there were a lot of officers and NCOs' who had served faithfully in at least one war and several incursions, such as Grenada, Panama, and Bosnia. They were getting out, and many of them and their older counterparts in retirement were dying. A death in the military community was not overlooked by the active force. As a result, those of us on active duty often had to serve on funeral details. I did it once.

It was for a master sergeant who had served in the last three wars. Politics notwithstanding, you could call Vietnam anything you wanted to, but if somebody was trying to kill me, I was at war. This man had seen action toward the end of the Korean Conflict, gone to Viet Nam, and wound up in Bosnia. Midway through his tour, he was the target for a sniper. The report read like he was the first one hit. He was probably dead before he hit the ground. They sent him home to his wife who was waiting for him in Columbus, the gate town for Benning.

When I got the call to report to the colonel's office, I had no idea what I was in for. He handed me a notebook full of rules. It was the dos and don'ts for the casualty assistance officer. I helped the widow plan the military funeral, got the sergeant a new uniform, and took her to the military lawyers who helped with his will and insurance. Everything went without a hitch till I had to present her the flag from his casket at the funeral.

The detail folded the flag. The firing squad fired the volley and, in the midst of taps, I realized I had to look this woman, this widow with three children, in the face and say something.

That scene was replaying itself in front of me as I prepared to answer Tracy.

"Tracy, do you know of anyone who might want to hurt Jeff."

She sat in stunned silence as what I really meant began to sink in. "Are you asking if I know anyone who might want to kill Jeff?" She looked beyond me and out the window of my office as she spoke. "How well did you know Jeff, Max? Did you talk about anything other than diving when you were together? I mean guy things."

"Guy things? Like baseball?" I asked.

"No, real guy things, like who's sleeping with whom. Did Jeff ever talk about women—other than me?"

Although it was Tracy sitting in front of me, I could picture Marge and the conversation we had on Friday. "No, Jeff didn't." That was not too big of a lie. Jeff had not actually spoken to me of other women. If Tracy had asked the same about Marge, I could not have answered the same way. "I think we better cut to the chase, Tracy."

"Good. If you think there was anything unusual about his death, please tell me." She hesitated, then turned back to face me. "And tell me why you think it. Is it speculation, or do you know something the police and I don't?"

I was an army captain in uniform, standing before

the widow again. I had to say something to make her believe her husband did not die in vain. My mouth was dry, my palms sweaty, my breath labored. "Jeff was an excellent diver. He was cautious with everything he did when we were together. I know he made many more dives at the Underwater Park than I did, and so he knew the lay of the land, so to speak. I just find it extremely difficult to believe he panicked at the first sign of trouble."

"So you think someone killed him?"

The widow was looking me in the eyes. I had to say something. The words, "On behalf of a grateful nation..." were running through my brain. "I think, with your permission, I'd like to look into the situation surrounding his death."

There was a long pause. I could hear her breathing.

"What do you think you'll find? And where do you start looking?"

"Both good questions. And I'm not certain on either. I'd like to start by going through any personal papers that the school may have boxed from his office." I poured us another cup of coffee from the old pot that sat slowly heating on the table near us. I handed one to her. "Did he have an office or any special room or place where he worked at home?"

"Are you looking for secrets? Things I might not know about? If so, I can put your mind at ease on a couple of points."

I thought back to my conversation with Marge and I doubted it.

"If I let you do this, and I haven't decided yet if I will, you'll, no doubt, see a side of Jeff—" She hesitated for a moment. "—and me, that you never dreamed possible." She stood and walked toward the door. She hesitated again and then turned back toward me. "Max, do you find me attractive?"

I know my mouth dropped open at that point. "Tracy, I—"

Tracy did not let me finish. "Jeff liked it when other men found me attractive. And I can't say it doesn't please me, either." She came back and sat down. "You said we should cut to the chase. Okay, let's do it. If you think there is something wrong with the official report about his death, I'll defer to you and let you see what you can find. But first, I think there are some things I need to tell you about the lifestyle Jeff and I lived." She paused, took a deep breath, then continued. "Are you familiar with the term 'Alternative Lifestyle'? In the sixties, we would have been called 'Swingers' or 'Wife Swappers.'"

Once again, I knew my mouth was open.

"Let me tell you the situation along with the whys before you pass judgment. Do I have your word on that?"

I nodded in agreement.

"I also want this to be in the strictest of confidence. Whether you take the case or not." She reached into her purse and pulled out a cigarette. Without asking, she flipped a lighter and inhaled deeply on the filtered cigarette. "Are we covered by some sort of client confidentiality? Like a lawyer or a priest?"

I got up and walked over to a three-drawer file cabinet in the far corner of the room. I opened the top drawer and pulled out a folder. From inside the folder I got one of my standard contracts.

I began to print her name in one of the blanks. "Do you have a dollar bill on you?"

"A dollar? Is that based on your ability or my net worth?"

The lady had a way with words. "That makes it legal. You've paid me, so this and anything else you tell me will be covered. Assuming you continue my services."

She rambled around in her purse until she found a

single bill and handed it to me. "Or you still want to after we finish talking."

I took the dollar and I gave her the contract and a pen. She signed.

"Jeff and I met in college. It was as close to love, or lust, at first sight as two people can get. We seemed to have almost everything in common. We were both going to become teachers. We liked the same music, movies, and books. My friends became his friends. His best friend married my old roommate. We were together constantly. I look back on it now and see that we were pre-destined for failure. We just had too much in common. There was nothing we did that didn't involve the other person. We almost became one person." Tracy handed me her empty coffee mug and nodded toward the pot.

I was filling the mug when the front door opened slightly and a familiar face filled the space. "Oh, I see you're busy, Colonel. I'll stop by later on. I got something to tell you, 'bout your friend—"

I cut George off before he could finish. Somehow, I felt he was about to say something I did not want the grieving widow to hear. "George. It's good to see you again." I gestured toward Tracy. "This is Mrs. Payton. Coach Payton's wife." I turned my attention to Tracy. "You've probably seen George around. He did some work for the school. He always spoke highly of Jeff."

George stood looking at Tracy in silence. He nodded at her. "I'm sorry to hear 'bout your husband, ma'am." George nodded again, gave me a knowing look, and left.

Tracy nodded. "Jeff hired him to do some yard work for us last year. Is he a friend of yours?"

"I never really gave it much thought, but, yes, George is a friend." I wanted to get her back to the information she was giving me about Jeff. "You were saying?"

"After four or five years, we realized we were tired of each other. We started to make new friends, mostly at school and in the education community. At home, the only two things we had in common anymore was our profession and sex. By then, Jeff was the assistant football coach and the counselor for the senior girls. If we had not been so dedicated to our professions—" She paused and took a long drag from the smoldering cigarette. I got the feeling she was not so much hooked on smoking as she was on the image it was supposed to portray. "—if Jeff had been a cab driver and I worked at the supermarket, I'm sure we would have gone our separate ways long ago."

I glanced at my watch. She had been in my office over an hour.

"About five years ago, I was on the verge of having an affair with a man I met at the dealership where they worked on my car. I had gone so far as to reserve a room at a little bed and breakfast place in the San Juan's. Then Jeff found out. In a way, I think I'm glad he did."

"This may sound like a really dumb question, but how can you be on the verge of having an affair? Either you are or you're not. It strikes me as like being a little bit pregnant. Till you actually are, you're not. That is how it works, isn't it?"

Tracy laughed for the first time that day. "Have you ever had an affair, Max? I know you guys count 'em differently, so even a one night stand counts." She sat back and waited.

"I'm sure I was not—" I began.

"This is not an essay question, Max. Yes or no. Did you ever cheat on your wife?"

I took a deep breath. I thought I was the one asking the hard questions. "Yes."

"See how difficult that was to admit. Wouldn't it

have been better if you could have come home from your little tryst on the side, opened the front door, and had dinner with the wife while the two of you discussed what happened? If there was no guilt, you could do that."

My conversation with Marge the previous day was making more sense by the minute. "I'm afraid I don't know anyone who is that magnanimous. Do you?"

"After I made my reservations at the bed and breakfast, they had a small fire and the cabin I was assigned was destroyed. They called to tell me and apologize. There would have been no problem if Jeff hadn't answered the phone and took the message. He confronted me, and we had the longest and most heart-wrenching talk we ever had." I saw it in her eyes as she drifted back to that conversation. "By the time we finished talking, we both agreed that we were together because of security and the occasional sex, which we both enjoyed. The security was the most important aspect of our marriage. We agreed that sex was a big part of our lives, and we missed it. I was about to have an affair, and Jeff said he already did. It was at that point we decided to find a way to keep the security of our marriage and enjoy the sex we both wanted. That's when we found out about the Final Frontier."

Tracy stubbed out the butt of her cigarette. She stood and began to walk around the office. I remained seated. I didn't know if she was through talking or just waiting for her second breath.

"The Final Frontier sounds like something out of a science fiction movie."

Tracy laughed aloud at my observation. "If you only knew how far out in space some of the people who go there seem to be, you'd know just how funny that really is."

She turned and sat on the corner of my desk. I almost

felt like one of her students. I doubt many of the students could appreciate the fact that, as she sat on the edge of the desk, she took on an extremely provocative pose. Her legs were crossed and her skirt slid a little higher than she probably allowed in the classroom. If Jeff liked to have men find her attractive, I was sure she had made him a very happy man.

"I think I may have told you enough for today, Max. If you could take me home, I would appreciate it. I've got someone coming over at five and I need to straighten up the house a little." She stood and went to the old oak rack where I had placed her coat when we came in.

"There is more that you plan to share with me, isn't there?"

"I'm going to see just how good you are as a private detective. See what you can find out about the Final Frontier."

Tracy put on her coat and, without waiting for me, walked out and stood on the sidewalk in front of my office. I followed her, locked the door, and we got into the Toyota for the ride to her house. As we pulled away from the parking lot, I saw George standing under the awning of the hardware store. He seemed to be watching for us to leave.

I knew the trip would take less than thirty minutes round trip. Allowing for bad traffic, in less than an hour I would be back in my office. As soon as I got back, the first thing I planned to do was look very closely at the card Marge had given me when she came to my office. If I was not completely mistaken it was from The Final Frontier, where I had agreed to meet her on Saturday evening.

# Chapter 9

Tracy barely spoke to me on the drive back to her house. When she did, it was about traffic, the weather, or any subject as far from our previous conversation as she could get. I pulled up in front of her house, cut the engine, and prepared to get out so I could go around and open her door. Before I got the transmission in park, she loosened her seatbelt, opened her door, and, with a quick smile in my direction, she was out.

As she was about to close the door, she leaned down to speak to me. "I'll call you in the next day or two to see what you've found and you can let me know if you're still interested."

Again she smiled and closed the door. I watched her till she was inside the house, then I drove back to my office.

The sun was making its way toward the Pacific when I opened my office door. Behind me, over the Olympic Peninsula, the still snow-covered mountains were tipped with an orange highlight. It was impossible not to notice it.

I had one message on the machine when I got to my desk. I hit the flashing button then scrambled to find a pen and paper in case there was something I needed to write down and save. There was a short pause before the person started talking. In the background, I heard what sounded like Latin or Salsa music. Then the voice came on. At first I didn't recognize it, but after a few words there was no doubt it was my new-found dive buddy.

"I wanted to call and thank you for a very pleasant afternoon dive. It's something I don't get to do as often as I like. I'm going to be at a little bed and breakfast called the St. George on Whidbey Island over the weekend. Since my husband will not be able to join me, I need a dive partner. If you're interested call me." She quickly gave her number and the line went dead. Most people stammered a bit when they got an answering machine. Not this lady. It was almost like she was reading a script. It was very precise and then she was gone. I looked at the number I had written and wondered if I would call it.

Diving with her was not on the immediate agenda. I opened my card file and pulled out the one Marge had given me. My initial instincts were correct. On the card was the same sunset that was playing itself out across the peninsula. Beneath the graphic was the name, FINAL FRONTIER. There was no address, but the phone number was listed as a twenty-four hour info hotline. I turned the card over and saw that Marge had given me an address in Richmond Beach, a small community on the water just south of Edmonds. She had also written a phone number, which I recognized as hers.

I pulled the coroner's report from my file cabinet and looked at the photos again. In death, Jeff looked like he had aged a decade. By the time the mortuary attendants finished with him, he had been returned to his rightful age. There were several cuts and scrapes on him. These were identified on the report as having come from the debris around the dive site. The thing that bothered me was the broken wrist. He must have been flailing about and gave one of the old pilings a hard smack to break it. All of these were secondary to the cause of death which was listed as a death by drowning. I was still holding the photos when the door opened and George entered.

"You alone, Colonel?"

"Yeah, sure, George. Come on in. What have you got on your mind?" I had known George long enough to know he didn't need to be primed with small talk.

"I still been worryin' 'bout the coach. I think you oughtta' look into why a man like him goes out one day and just up and drowns. Ain't right and you know it. If he was my friend, I know I'd be looking all 'round that high school to see if any of them students know anything." George took his regular seat on the windowsill.

"What makes you think one of the kids at school had anything to do with it?" I grabbed the coffee pot and walked to the back room where I filled it with water and prepared to make a fresh pot.

George waited until I returned before he replied. "One of 'em was with him when he died. It was that boy that was the football quarterback last year." He stopped to think for a second. "He coulda' been from the year before, but I know he was the one. And them little girls—"

I stopped George in mid-sentence. "What 'little girls' George? What are you talking about?"

"If you ever went down there after school, you'd know. Every afternoon, I'd see him come out of the building with a different one. Didn't matter to him if they was black or white, tall or short. It was a different one nearly every day. I only seen him with the same one a couple of times. Seen her with that boy that was with him when he died, too."

I listened to George. I knew he worked at the school occasionally, and he must have seen Jeff when he finished with his counseling job at the end of the school day.

Tracy mentioned that Jeff was working with the senior girls as a counselor. Even so, George might have seen something the rest of us did not. "What exactly did you see, George? Did Coach Payton ever leave with any of the girls?

"I never said he did. All I said was the way they stood there and talked—well, I wouldn't want none of my chil'ren actin' like that with no man old enough to be their daddy."

I was about to respond to him when I heard the sirens of an aid vehicle echo through the streets as one pulled out from the fire station around the corner. Several times a day, they came down in front of the shop as they made their way through the city. This one was headed up the hill from the waterfront. At least it wasn't another diver in trouble.

"When Coach Payton's wife came in here today, I agreed to look into his death. At some point, I know I'll want to talk to you about him and the kids you saw him with at school."

"So you don't think it was no accident neither." George seemed to take a bit of pleasure in his rationale for my looking into Jeff's death. He leaned back on his ledge-side seat and smiled. "I think you'll find out what really happened."

He stood and poured the coffee into a large plastic mug he pulled from a place where he had secured it in his coat pocket. Mug in hand, George opened the door and exited into the now-darkened streets.

I left the office and went to my apartment. I had a place not far from downtown. It was in a quiet part of the city. I found the duplex which I now rented when I was literally put on the street after my divorce. We had to sell the house and my part of the small profit was not enough to make a decent down payment on another one. Since then, I'd gotten used to not having to worry about leaky plumbing, too-old appliances, and taxes that bordered on obscene in this county.

My place was decorated for comfort, not speed. My needs had always been simple. I bought what I liked and used what I bought. The one concession I made was a large screen plasma television. I didn't watch a lot of sports but the combination of a good sound system and the screen made the videos I rented look like I was in the theater.

I parked in the driveway, pulled the mail from my box, and opened the front door. I didn't think I'd ever get used to the split second loneliness that washed over me each time I opened the door and realized there was no one there but me. That was generally the time I wished I could start over again. I'd have my daughters waiting inside. As soon as I opened the door, they'd come running to tell me who had been mean to whom that day. I'd swear I was more of a referee than a father, but after a while they'd kiss and make up. Since my wife worked some of the time, we usually shared kitchen duty. My dinner now usually consisted of anything that came in a box or something that could be micro waved.

I hit the light switch and the room came to life. I passed through the black hole. For the first time in many weeks, I went to the cabinet where I kept my few bottles of liquor and poured a tall gin and tonic. I knew I had fresh limes in the refrigerator, so I gave into the desire and made the drink.

With drink in hand, I went to the living room and sat on the couch while I read my mail. I held at least half a pound of paper that I found in my mailbox. Only one piece had first class postage on it. The remainder was advertisements and bulk-rate announcements that I had been selected to win a trip somewhere. All I had to do was spend a day with a real estate sales rep trying to sell me a piece of land. At the end of the day, I'd realize the prize was a certificate entitling me to stay at a fleabag motel if I paid the airfare. Thank you, no. They went into the recycle bin, unopened.

I called Hart's and left a message for Leigh to call me when she had a break. We had an unwritten rule between us. Unless she answered the phone, I never asked to speak to her. When she called my office to speak to me, her first words were, "Are we alone?"

If I had someone with me, I never had to try to talk around them. That was a system that worked for us.

While I waited for her to return my call, I picked up the clicker for the television and hit the button, turning the large screen from black to full color. It was still preset to the news station where I had been watching the last time it was activated. It was more for noise than entertainment. I resisted the urge to take a quick ride through the channels and lay the clicker on the end table.

I reached into my pocket and extracted the card Marge had given me. I turned it over to where she had written the number and picked up the phone to dial it. *If I dial the number, I'm in*, I thought as I looked at it. Up to this point, I was doing all this out of a sense of...of what? Of honor to Jeff, a man whom I did not know all that well but liked anyway? Perhaps it was one of curiosity. How did Jeff die? Could it have been prevented? Was it a mistake I was likely to make if I went diving the park again? I thought it was "all of the above" and "none of the above" at the same time. I was in a large puzzle, and I was being handed the pieces one at a time. That was not so unusual, but I was asking myself to assemble them without the benefit of having seen the box lid with the completed puzzle on it. I was still holding the card when the phone rang.

"Hello."

"Hi, Kelly said you called."

I could hear the late night crowd at Hart's as they finished their dinner and moved to the bar. "Yeah, I did. What's your schedule this weekend? I may have to go out Saturday night."

Leigh was using the pay phone in the ladies room. "I'm here five till closing on Saturday. But I've got Sunday off if that'll help."

"I don't know yet." I turned the card over and re-read the notice about the twenty-four-hour info line. "It may have to be on Saturday. I'll let you know."

"Gotta go, see you tonight?"

"I'll be there. I may just wait in the parking lot. If I do, I'll call."

I sometimes waited for her in the lot rather than going inside. That way, I didn't have to worry about making small talk with the last customers or some of the other people waiting there. With at least four hours till I met her, I could take a nap, watch television, or—I looked again at the card. Or I could step to the edge of the board and jump. There was a pool below me. It was filled with unanswered questions, perhaps even unanswerable questions, about Jeff. Also swimming about in the murky waters was his attractive widow Tracy. Somewhere I would find Marge; at least three young girls from the high school; Nelson Roberts, his dive partner that fateful day; and a black man, known to everyone in town as Crazy George, who was convinced Jeff didn't die by accident.

What the hell? I picked up the phone and dialed.

# CHAPTER 10

The phone was answered on the third ring. I usually let a phone ring four times before I give up. Most people set their machines to answer at five rings. If they haven't picked up by four, they're either not home or they want to hear a voice and then decide if they'll pick up in person.

"Hello."

"Hi, this is Max. Is this Marge?" Her voice sounded deeper on the phone. It could have been something she did or it may have been natural. Either way, it had a certain sexiness to it.

"Oh, hi, Max. I'm glad you called. I was beginning to wonder if you took what I said seriously." She lost her whiskey voice when she started a normal conversation.

I guessed she had an answering voice and a talking voice. I was getting both.

"I took it very seriously. It's just that I didn't know if I would have any involvement in an investigation of Jeff's death."

"And now you do?"

"I'm beginning to think so."

"Did Tracy hire you?"

I heard the flick of a lighter and then the long exhaling as Marge let go of a lung full of smoke. "I'm not at liberty to divulge the name of my client." I had to say that even though she knew who hired me.

"A man of mystery and integrity. I think I like that, Mister Maxwell." There was a long pause. "What did Tracy tell you?"

"About what in specific? We discussed a lot of things."

"Mister Maxwell, you need to know one thing right now. Of all the people you're gonna talk to who knew Jeff, I'm the only one you don't have to play games with."

This was a conversation I did not want to have over the phone. I tried to turn the focus to something more appropriate for the telephone. "This place you want to meet at on Saturday, what exactly is it?"

She laughed before she answered. "You'll either think you've died and gone to heaven or you've gone straight to the depths of hell." She hesitated for that to sink in. "I'd suggest you come alone. This is not a place to bring your lady friend till you've checked it out first."

I heard her take a long pull on her cigarette.

"I'll have to say you've gotten my curiosity up. Is there anything special I should know or do prior to coming?"

Marge was laughing, almost hysterically. She calmed down a moment then she came back to the phone. "If you only knew how funny what you just said was, Mister Maxwell. No, don't do anything to prepare. Just stay aroused. You've got the address. I think that will be the first place you need to start looking if you're serious about finding out what really happened to Jeff."

"Will your husband be there?"

"Trust me, Barry wouldn't miss a Saturday night at the Frontier to attend his own mother's funeral. Oh, he'll be there, all right. I might even be able to stop Barry long enough to introduce him to you if you like."

Considering her allegation that he might be involved in Jeff's death, I thought that would be a very good idea. We made a small amount of polite talk in order to make us both feel proper about my calling her, and then I broke off the conversation.

When I pushed the button on the phone, terminating the conversation, I placed it on the table near the big chair where I normally sat and did whatever it was I did when I was alone. Sometimes it was to watch television. More likely it was to read or simply sit and listen to the jazz station I managed to find on my FM radio one day. As I put the phone down, I picked up a book I had been reading off and on for the last couple of weeks.

I seemed to read several books on a topic then rapidly changed interests and went to something else. I'd found myself reading books on near-death experiences, the ancient Druids and Stonehenge, and books tied to specials on nature and the environment. My fiction favorites were mysteries but I usually left those for late at night when I awakened and couldn't go back to sleep. My interest for the last few months had been the Civil War. I picked up my book on General Longstreet, which was lying on the table beside the chair, and began to read.

The book had fallen to the floor when the street noise awakened me. A car was racing its engine outside on the street. I remembered my days of fast cars and loud engines. Some things never changed. I had been in such a deep sleep it took a moment for me to come completely awake. I shook my head to clear the cobwebs and looked at the clock on the DVD player. As usual, it was blinking twelve o'clock. I picked up the book, placed it back on the table, and turned off the lamp I had used to read and ultimately used for a night light. When I looked at my watch, I saw it was time to go get Leigh. I walked to my front door and opened it.

The first shot ripped into the doorframe as I was about to exit. My first reaction was to drop. It might have been a lifesaving response, since as I dropped, I heard the CRACK as the second round passed overhead and through the center of the open doorway. If I had been still standing there, I was sure it would have been just as likely to pass through my middle. I rolled to the side of the steps leading to the street and dropped to the ground. My first thought was that I had a pistol and I could have returned the fire, except for one little problem. My gun was in a drawer in my apartment, and I was groveling around on the ground outside.

I heard the car speed away. I could only assume it was both the same car that held the shooter and was the one revving its engine, enticing me to open my front door out of curiosity. Although the curiosity factor did not work, their timing was almost perfect. They came just as I needed to leave to go to see Leigh. Was that a coincidence? I wouldn't find out lying on the ground.

Several nearby neighbors had come outside to see what the noise was all about. My closest neighbor was an old retired tugboat captain named Dan. He had lived in the area since when the city had been considered country. When he came out of his place, he was holding a well-smoked black briar pipe.

"What-the-hell was that? Kids throwing firecrackers again? Little bastard's oughtta be put in jail." He noticed me brushing the light dirt from my pants. "What happened to you? They scare you enough to make you jump into the flower bed?"

He stepped into the light from my place and saw the splintered doorjamb. "Son of a bitch! You must be doin' a good job at something. Somebody's tryin' to kill your ass." He stepped slightly and cautiously out of the full light from my living room.

"No, it's okay, Dan. I'm fine. Thanks for askin'." I turned to look at the door. The slug was mushroomed into the right side of the doorjamb. I could see a small part of the lead protruding from the wood.

"Didn't they teach you in the army that a miss was as good as a mile?" Dan had evidently assumed I was not going to draw any more fire so he came to stand beside me. "I remember when we were getting ready to invade Japan. They took us off of the cargo ships and—"

"Dan, I really appreciate the philosophy lesson but I need to check out my apartment to see if anything was broken. I know at least one round came inside." I stepped around him and entered the room. He followed.

I immediately saw where the second round had sped through my living space. It had passed through the shade on the lamp I had been using to read the Longstreet book. After leaving the lampshade, it hit the wall near my stereo. I smelled Dan's pipe as he fired it up behind me.

"Whatcha' working on, Max? Some husband find out you got pictures of him dippin' his pen at work?"

Before I could answer, I heard a car door slam. It was the Edmonds PD.

"Everything okay, Colonel?"

When I turned toward the voice, it was Gunny.

"How'd you get stuck with the night shift, Gunny?" I supposed one of my neighbors who was not as curious as Dan simply called the police.

"I traded shifts so I could take a couple of days off to visit my daughter in Oregon." He looked around the room. "What seems to be the problem? We got a call about—"

Before he could finish, Dan broke in. "Somebody tried to shoot ol' Max. Either they didn't try too hard, or they can't shoot worth a shit. Didn't hit nothin' but his doorjamb and the wall. Hell, I can do better than that. And I'm over eighty." Dan was still puffing on his pipe when he walked back to his apartment.

"I didn't know you and Dan were such good friends." Gunny laughed as he pulled out a notebook to do his report. "First things first. Are you okay?"

"I'm fine. I think whoever it was just got off two shots. One hit the doorjamb and the other passed through the place. It's in the wall over there." I pointed to the point of entry.

Gunny walked over to the hole. "I'd say a thirty-eight. Any idea who might have been on the other end of it?"

"Not a clue." I checked my watch. It was time to leave. "I'm not working on anything that would cause this kind of reaction."

I couldn't imagine anyone from the mall who might be stealing from the gift shop trying to shoot me. It was way too early for them. Unless the owner had mentioned my name, no one even knew me.

That left two choices if it was intentional. It was someone from a previous case or—or it had to do with Jeff's death. That was a hell of a choice but it was all I could come up with.

"If you don't mind, I'd just as soon let this drop. I know you've got enough other paperwork to do. You don't need a random drive-by in Edmonds. Could make property values drop like a stone." I was easing Gunny toward the door, and he knew it.

"It's your call, Colonel. You say it was kids throwing firecrackers, that's good enough for me. That's what the initial call to nine-one-one said it was, too." He folded the cover over on his notebook and put it back in his pocket. "I can take care of it from the call-in report."

"Works for me, Gunny. If I determine it was more than that, I'll call you."

He began to walk back toward his cruiser. I followed. "Make certain you do. If it went to one of the suits like Fitzgerald, they might not understand why there wasn't a paper trail from this point on."

"Not to worry. You'll be the first one called if necessary."

He opened his door, pulled his nightstick from his belt, placed it on the seat, and slid gracefully into the car.

I watched him pull away from the curb, then I went back inside and closed up my place.

The drive to Hart's took less than ten minutes. I arrived just as the elevator opened and Leigh and one of the waitresses exited into the night air. The elevator for Hart's was designed to be used by the kitchen. It went from ground level to the first floor and opened next to the kitchen. When another restaurant in town was successfully sued by a wheelchair patron for failure to provide handicap access, the elevator was quickly converted. It had hauled so much fish in its previous usage; it was almost a year before a customer did not have to hold his or her nose on the ride.

Leigh watched the other woman walk to her car, then she came to where I was sitting. As she approached, I got out and went to open the door for her. She gave me a quick kiss as she virtually dropped into the seat. "Take me home. I'm beat."

She had her hair tied with a little rubber band thing. She removed it and shook her head so her hair flipped around. I reached across and ran my hand through it. It felt soft and silky.

"Busy night, huh?"

She had left her car in the shop for a new set of tires, so there was no choice of cars tonight.

"We had a birthday party come in that the day hostess had forgotten to put on the book. There were fourteen people we had to find places for." She leaned into the seat as she began to relax.

"And of course you gathered the troops together to do another sterling job. As usual."

"Naturally. It's my nature to be an organizer. Sometimes I think I should run for president. If I did, I'd let you be vice president."

"Second-in-command? Never!"

She leaned toward me and gave me another kiss. This was a good sign. "No, you'd be *vice* president. You'd be in charge of vice."

"That's one of every man's three fantasies, you know."

"I'm afraid to even ask what the other two might be." She turned serious. "What did you do today? Did you find out about Saturday? I know I can't get off."

I stopped at a red light and waited for it to turn. Sometimes, in the wee hours of the early morning, I treated red lights as stop signs. I waited full turn for that one. It turned green, and I pulled away. "Looks like it's got to be on Saturday night. I don't know how long it'll take, so I'll call you on Sunday. Just sleep in and we'll do something in the afternoon."

I walked Leigh to her door; made certain she got inside, and left. I told her to call me when she awakened the next morning, and I would come get her and drive her back to the tire store to pick up her car.

I took my time driving back to the duplex. Once I got there, I checked it out from the street and then circled the block several times prior to pulling into my parking place. I did not see the car that drew me out of my place earlier in the evening. It was probably the same one that held the shooter.

I wanted it to be some gang banger undergoing an initiation where he or she had to fire a couple of shots at a house and the deal was done. I also wanted there to be a Santa Clause and an Easter Bunny.

When I got home, I saw all the lights were out in my neighbors' apartments and condos. I couldn't help but take a few cautious steps from the car to the light from the front of the building before I felt like I might make it without a repeat of the earlier incident. Ten minutes later, I was in bed and as fast asleep as I can get.

It was a little after seven when I awakened. I got up, took a shower, shaved, and left for the Treetopper. After my usual breakfast, I called Tracy. It was almost nine by then.

"Tracy, its Max. I was wondering if I could drop by sometime this morning." In the background of the Treetopper, the jukebox was already cranked up and going. The current selection playing made it difficult to hear her over the sound of some lovesick cowboy truck-driving outlaw and his guitar.

"Sure. Just give me time to get dressed. I'm running a little late today."

We agreed to meet at her house at ten. With an hour to kill, I had enough time to drive to the high school. At least I got as far as the little restaurant across the street from it. I pulled into their parking lot, parked the Four Runner, and went inside.

My coffee consumption for the day had already exceeded the maximum allowance but I needed to have a reason for sitting in the booth by the window overlooking the school.

I popped quarters into the coin slot on the paper box and got a USA TODAY. With coffee and a newspaper, I was ready to sit there and do something. Unfortunately, I hadn't quite decided what it was I was going to do.

The old man who ran the place was cleaning a table next to mine. "It was quite a loss when Coach Payton died, wasn't it?" I asked to get his reaction.

"Yeah, the kids really took it hard. Especially some of the young girls he was working with. We got one that comes in here almost every day. She just sits and talks about him all the time. Yes, sir, she took it real hard." He gave the table another swipe with the cloth and went back to the kitchen. Across the street, a car full of kids, who were probably cutting class, peeled out of the parking lot and ignored the school zone speed limits as they sped away.

The man finished wiping the tables and came to stand beside me. It was a not-too-subtle indication that if I was going to occupy a chair I had better be prepared to spend some money.

Out of habit, I glanced at the menu board. It was much too early for a hamburger and fries, so I ordered another cup of coffee and took a chance that he wouldn't have one when I asked if he had a muffin of some type. Fortunately, he didn't.

I watched the street across from me as students came and went from the school. I wasn't not certain I knew what or who I was looking for but I managed to kill almost an hour with the paper and two more cups of coffee. I had enough caffeine to stay awake for a week. When I got up to leave, I put three dollars on the table. I had managed to stay there until time to go to meet Tracy.

I knocked on Tracy's front door at exactly ten. From inside, I heard the deep throaty chimes of a grandfather clock as it struck the time. The last strike was still vibrating when she opened the door.

Jeff had been dead ten days. Her period of mourning was over, from the looks of her. She was wearing a very tight pair of jeans, a white tee shirt, and sandals. Her hair was pulled back and tied with a bright colored ribbon. Tracy's eyes sparkled when she spoke. "Max, please come in." She took me gently by the arm and led me inside.

"This is not too early, is it?"

"Not for me. I'm a morning person. Jeff always was a night person, but the mornings are the best for me. Can I make you a cup of coffee?" She indicated I should sit on the couch in the living room while she went into the next room to get her coffee. She quickly returned and took a seat on the other end of the couch. "So? Did you give sufficient thought to what I said about Jeff and me?"

"I did."

She took her time as she continued to sip coffee. "And you've decided to...to what, Max? Is our relationship that of an employer and her employee?"

"Officially and legally, yes it is. But I'd also like to think I'm doing this for Jeff, too."

"I can live with that. Where do we begin?"

"I wanted to look at any papers Jeff might have had here at the house and any you picked up from his office at school. Will that be a problem?"

"Not at all. I've got the things from his office at school in the garage. There were only three boxes. The rest of the stuff was school property. Books, student records, and evaluations. Stuff like that. The school still has the boxes with that stuff in them." She stood and beckoned for me to follow. "As for things here at the house, I don't think you'll find anything. He did some work here but, mostly, it was at school. That was one thing I admired about him. He always left his work at work. He seldom brought it home." We went into a small room about the size of a child's bedroom. "This is what you would call his office. You're welcome to go through everything here. I'll be in the den if you need anything. I'm trying to catch up on some reading so I can return to school next week."

I waited until she was out of the room before I started to look through the desk drawers. I dreaded the next search. On the desk was his computer. I had enough problems with my own computer, so I knew my limits with trying to get into his. There were people in Seattle who worked for Microsoft who could turn on his computer, hit a few keys, and bring up everything he had ever written, even though he thought he had deleted it. I was just the opposite. When I wrote something and sent it to the printer, it usually wound up in Botswana or some other equally exotic place. Anywhere except the printer, which was sitting on a table three feet away.

I sat down and looked at the machine. Two green lights looked back at me. He had a box of discs sitting on a shelf above the monitor. I reached for it and opened the dark plastic lid. Inside were about thirty discs with paper labels indicating they were school records, tax records, and general correspondence. I was thumbing through them when the small red paper dot affixed to one caught my eye.

Since none of the others had red dots, or dots of any other color, I felt certain this one meant something special. Unfortunately, I could not just hold it up to the light or lean it against the monitor and see what was on the disc, so I did the next best thing. I slipped it into my pocket, and began to look closely at the remainder of the office.

Jeff was a very neat person. Almost everything in the desk drawers had a place and was in that place. Letters were filed, bills had rubber bands around them, and even the pencils were not lying loose in the drawers. He had a system and he used it. His system also included taping a small key to the bottom of the main drawer of the desk.

When I found it, I slipped it into my pocket. What it meant would be determined when I found what it fit.

In the top drawer, I found an address book. I'd seen enough to know when something was written in code in a book like this. Jeff's had lots of code. A series of numbers written across the bottom of a card could indicate an address, a home phone number, or a not-to-be-forgotten date. I found several cards with these notations. The names on the cards were either one letter and a last name or non-specific gender names like Pat or Jo.

I didn't think I'd find anything else until I opened the closet and started to look through a large cardboard box in the corner under a pile of magazines. It was there I found the photos.

In almost any other country in the world you could buy locally produced porno pictures. It was not something that was unique to the United States. I'd seen my share or more over the years in the army, but I never saw any with someone in the picture I recognized. As soon as I flipped through the photos, I knew Jeff was one of the men in the action shots. I had looked at five or six when I got my second shock for the day. I immediately recognized one of the women in the photos. There were two shots of her in a large swimming pool. Another couple was with her. In one photo, the two women were sitting on the edge of the pool. There was a man between them. All were facing the camera and all were completely nude. I did not recognize the other man but the red-haired women in the picture looked quite familiar. I thought it might be wishful thinking until I finally recognized her. There was no doubt the woman on the right was Tracy.

In the next photo, the man was on top of a woman. They were having sex. It was not hard to determine who he was with, since the red-haired woman was sitting beside him and watching. By the time, I had looked at all the photos, I had seen Jeff and Tracy and the other couple in any number of different combinations.

If these were not too well hidden in the closet, I couldn't imagine what would be in the box that Jeff thought enough of to keep locked. Like the key, I slipped the photos in my pocket.

I left the room and walked toward the den where Tracy was reading. She barely looked up as she spoke. "Did you find anything?"

"Bits and pieces. I'm not sure what I'm looking for so it's difficult to know when I've found it." I had my hand in my coat pocket. I felt the heat from the photos. "I'd like to take a look at the boxes from school. Do you mind?"

Without answering, Tracy slowly unwrapped herself from the couch where she sat with her legs doubled beneath her. "They're out here in the garage." She led the way through the house to the attached two-car garage.

Unlike most garages I'd seen and all that I'd owned, this one was actually clean and uncluttered enough to get a car inside. Shelves lined one wall. Above the shelves were three cabinets with padlocks on them. Tracy walked to the far corner and stood looking down at three large file boxes sitting on the floor.

"The school packed the boxes. You're the first to see them since they were delivered to me." She continued to look at them. "He was a person who saved everything but it was all put in some type of order. You'd be surprised how much more you can keep if you don't let it turn to clutter." She shifted her focus from the boxes to me. "I'll bet you have a lot of clutter in your life, Max." Without elaboration or allowing me to answer, she returned to the inside of the house.

I opened the first box and found it filled with personal books and the other items one had in an office. There were two photos of Tracy and Jeff. One was taken during a ski trip. The other was a formal portrait. I couldn't believe the woman smiling back at the camera in those two photos was the same as the one in the photos in my jacket pocket.

The second box held Jeff's desk calendar and appointment book. I compared several dates on both and they were the same. He had made notations for after school teachers meetings, one appointment with the parents of one of his students, and a meeting with someone listed only as Doc. It was in the appointment book but not the calendar so I had to assume it took place off school grounds.

I found a small locked metal box that was used to hold five-by-eight-inch file cards. I took the key from my pocket and tried it. With a quick turn of the key, the box opened. Dividers had been placed in the box so the three-by-five-inch lined cards were in order. I flipped through the first few letters of the alphabet and was about to close it when I got to the letter L. There was a card for a person named Lewis. There was no first name or address, but the phone number indicated a local exchange. I wouldn't have given that a second look if I had not pulled out the card and the small envelope behind it. I didn't know what I was looking for, so I looked at everything. That was how I found the photos of the nude girls.

# CHAPTER 11

The file box sat on the seat next to me as I drove back to my office. I had taken it along with the calendar, appointment book, and another book that might prove to be some type of diary when I had a chance to read it. After finding the photos, I dug a bit more until I found a school student directory. I slipped it into the stack of things I wanted. I went back into the house and asked Tracy if I could take a few items back to my office. She voiced no concern, so I quickly packed the pieces into a cardboard box I found in the garage and left.

When I got back to my office, I unloaded the contents of the box on my desk. I noticed the light blinking on my phone, so I pushed the button and picked up a pen in order to write any messages I might have.

The first one was from Gunny at the police department. The second was my still un-named female visitor from the high school. "Mister Maxwell—I'd like to came back and talk to you. This time, it'll be different." I could hear the sound of the kids in the hallway as they almost drowned her out. "I'll—I'll call you later today." The third call was from the same place. I heard the kids again. Before the caller could say anything, I heard another voice very close by. "Cathy, I've been looking—"

At that point, the line went dead. It was a safe bet that my mystery caller was named Cathy.

I placed the metal box with the cards on my desk. I started with the first letter of the alphabet and worked my way to the end. I found a small envelope behind five additional cards. All but one had professional quality photographs of a partially nude young girl. I lay that one aside. They were all taken in the same room. It was Jeff's office at school. The photos were shots of the girls with bared breasts in a variety of poses with an article of clothing or their hands covering themselves so they were not completely nude. All of their faces were turned away from the camera, so none were identifiable. The exception was the one I had placed by itself.

I thought of my own two daughters as I looked at it. How would this young girl's father feel if he knew I was holding a photo of his completely naked daughter standing, proudly facing the camera and the man behind it?

I suddenly didn't like myself very much for looking at the photos. I liked the man who took them even less. It was safe to assume that man was Jeff.

I placed the cards and the photos face down on my desk. I stood up and walked outside into the limited sunlight still available. I wanted some clean air. When I'd held the photos, I felt like I was breathing the same air as the person who took them. That air hurt.

After a minute on the street, I went back inside. I kept the photos turned over and looked at the name cards I found with each. I took the first one named Lewis and I began to go through the school directory until I found a name that matched the name and phone number on the card.

Each of the photos was of students and all lived in areas closely surrounding the school.

I had just finished writing the last name and address

when the phone rang. It was a welcome opportunity to turn my attention to something else.

"Max here."

"Mister Maxwell. I called you earlier today."

It was my caller from the school. This time, she must have been using a phone away from school since I did not hear the normal background noises.

"Oh, hi, Cathy. You sound like you're away from school now. It's much quieter." I figured what the hell, it might make her tell me what was on her mind.

"Yeah, I'm across—" She stopped in mid-sentence. "How'd you find out my name? I—I didn't tell—"

"I'm a detective. That's what I do. I find out things about people. Some of the things I find are easy, some are not. Like finding out what you want to tell me. I can't do that on my own. You've got to help." I waited to see how she would respond.

"I'm sorry. I didn't mean to string you along. It's just that, well—I didn't want to get anyone in trouble."

"Nobody's gonna get into trouble. You can tell me anything you like, and I promise I won't do anything you don't want me to do." She was silent on the other end of the line. "Cathy? You still there?"

"I'm here. I guess I can talk to you. I'm just so mixed up right now. You know, with all that's happened."

"I know. These can be some rough times, especially if you don't have anyone you can talk to." I hesitated, then. "Why don't we meet someplace where you feel comfortable talking to me. Maybe the library. It's just up the street. I can be there in ten minutes." I wanted an excuse to leave the photos that I had on my desk.

"Okay, but in an hour. I'll have to go by my house first. There are some tables in the back of the library. I'll meet you there." She replaced the phone on its cradle and the line began to buzz as she broke the connection.

I held the phone for a moment, then I dialed the Edmonds Police Department. "Is Officer Reed available or may I leave a message. I'm returning his call."

The operator put me on hold. The background music was from a local radio station, and I made it through two commercials for appliances before Gunny picked up the phone.

"Officer Reed here. May I help you?"

"Gunny, its Max. You called and left a message for me."

"Oh, yeah, Colonel. We got a possible ID on the shooter's car. It may have been a small black job. Maybe a CRX or a Toyota. Somebody was out walking a dog when one nearly ran over the mutt about a block from your place. The lady didn't get a license or anything but she said there was only one person in it."

"I'll bet her description of the driver would fit half the people in town, too."

"You got it. White male wearing a ball cap. Doesn't narrow it down too much, does it?" I heard Gunny laugh at the irony of his own comment.

"I can't think of anyone who fits that description that jumps to my mind but I appreciate the info. This is still off the report sheet, isn't it?" I didn't want the near death experience of a dog trying to take a dump to get the incident in the official reports.

"Not to worry. Our residents are just like those everywhere. If it don't happen to them, it don't concern 'em. None of your neighbors has said anything. As long as they don't—"

He didn't have to finish. I knew he was taking a chance. If anyone reported it and the chief asked to see the report from the investigating officer, Gunny would have to do an admirable job of tap dancing to keep ahead of a real ass chewing. As soon as I hung up with Gunny, I dialed the owner of the store at the mall. I wanted to ask him about the value of his missing items. One of his employees told me he was en route to the store in Tacoma. I thanked her and terminated the call.

When I finished with that call, I picked up a note pad and headed for the door. It was a five-minute walk to the city library. The air felt good. It had a slight sting to it as the wind blew up Main Street from the Sound.

As I entered the automatic doors, I remembered the small library in my hometown. It was in the center of town in a building that had once been a feed store. The wood floors were stained dark from years of farmers tracking in and out, buying feed and seed for their farms. The checkout desk was the same one used by the previous business. It was so high some of the little children couldn't even see over it to check out their books. One wall held the children's section. The adult books covered the remaining sidewall and the back section. The librarian, Miss Porter, whom we all thought was old enough to have witnessed the American Revolution, was adamant about not letting us near the adult section until we were twelve.

To further protect us, the adult section had a blue stripe painted across the front edge of one shelf. The line was on the shelf next to the top and was over the head of almost everyone in town under the age of twelve. This was Miss Porter's failsafe system. If you were under the line, you were in deep trouble.

We had heard rumors there were books in that section with swear words in them. Twelve couldn't come fast enough.

I entered the library and went straight to the back. Cathy was already waiting at a table. She had a small pile of books in front of her. I'd bet Miss Porter would do a back flip in her grave if she could thumb through half the books in the children's section today.

I walked slowly toward the table. "You're early. Or am I late?" I placed my hand on the back of a chair. "Mind if I sit?"

"No. I mean, no, I don't mind."

There was an innocence about her that I knew was genuine. She looked up and smiled.

I held out my hand. "Let's start fresh. I'm Max. You must be Cathy."

She took my hand in an awkward shake. "Yes. Yes, I am."

I slid the chair back from the table and took a seat. I wanted to let her start talking first. "I know this has all been very difficult on you and many of the others at the school." I watched her nod in agreement. "How can I help? What can I do?"

"Uh, I guess I'm kinda worried about Patti Sherman. She was really…uh…really close, to Jeff, to Coach Payton."

Patti Sherman. I recalled the name. It was the last photo I found in his locked file box. The student directory gave her address as a mere three streets away from where Jeff and Tracy lived.

I remembered Patti Sherman as the young woman standing, almost defiantly, looking at the camera as it captured her nakedness. I had to agree with Cathy. Patti did seem rather close to Jeff. "What do you mean by 'close,' Cathy?"

She stammered a bit as she nervously answered. "He was her counselor, ya know. He was trying to help her get in this school after she graduated. It was something she really wanted. Nelson didn't like it but—" Once she loosened up she ran at full speed.

"Slow down a bit. I need to understand everything

you're telling me and I'm afraid I don't." I opened my notebook. "I want to take a few notes."

"You're not going to mention my name are you?"

"Not if you ask me not to." I made a notation of the time and location on the first line. "Now, tell me what kind of school Patti wants to go to and why Nelson doesn't like it."

"Do you know Nelson?"

"I don't know him personally. Should I?"

"He's Patti's boyfriend. She calls him her fiancé, but I don't think he's given her a ring or anything." Cathy was interrupted when a girl from school stopped by the table and asked her about an upcoming test in English. She hardly paid any attention to me as I busied myself with one of the books Cathy had on the table.

"Tell me about how Jeff was helping Patti," I asked when the other girl left. "What was he doing for her?"

"At school, we have counselors who are supposed to help us with finding a job after we graduate or a college or scholarships and stuff like that. Jeff had Patti. I've got Mrs. Gables. She's good but I'm not sure what I want to do yet."

"What was Patti trying to do, Cathy?"

Cathy looked down and blushed slightly. "I'm sorry. You don't want to hear about me. We're here to talk about Patti."

There was so much pain in her voice I could feel it across the table.

"Patti is one of the prettiest girls in school. She always wanted to be a model or actress. Jeff was trying to help her. He had a friend in Portland he wanted her to meet. He had something to do with the movies." She looked at me and smiled. "Patti had the second lead in the school play last year. She could've had the lead this year except—" She stopped and looked down at her books.

"Except what, Cathy?"

"Nelson was jealous of her being in the play. It was all right last year when he was there, but with him at Community College now, he didn't want her to do it."

I reached in my pocket and pulled out a small piece of paper. I had written the names of the other girls whose photos I found on it. "Do you know any of these girls, Cathy?" I read the names to her.

"I've got classes with two of 'em. Is that what you mean?"

"Perhaps. What else do you know about them?"

She began to fidget with the books in front of her. I reached across the table and placed my hand on the book to stop her from moving it. "Anything else?"

"They all have—had—Jeff for their counselor."

"And?" I felt there was more.

"I know Donna and Gail wanted to go to modeling school."

"Like Patti?"

"Yes, sir. Like Patti." Cathy was looking down at the pen in her hand. "You won't tell them I said anything? Will you? You promised."

I shook my head. "Your secret is safe with me."

As I stood to leave, I saw a young girl who was expected to become an adult in a few months simply because she walked across a stage and somebody placed a diploma in her hand.

She wasn't ready for it, and I couldn't do anything to slow down the process. I walked away, feeling like a failure.

Since I wasn't charging Tracy anything yet and my landlord wouldn't accept excuses instead of a rent check, I took a two-day job for a group of attorneys. I served several sets of divorce papers and various other subpoenas throughout the county. It was a fairly easy way to make rent money, and I usually worked a few days for them every month.

By Friday afternoon, I had finished so I went to an afternoon movie. That was something else I did as frequently as I could. I didn't like films with a message or a moral. I wanted to get a soda, a bag of popcorn, and shift into neutral for two hours. I picked a mindless comedy, and it worked.

After the movie, I went home, gathered all my dirty clothes, and went to the laundromat, where I spent another mindless hour.

The sounds of a gunfight awakened me on Saturday morning. It took a second to realize it was on the still-playing television. Two cowboys with twenty shooters were going at it. I looked at my clock. It was six-thirty. I was awake with nothing to do for another six hours.

I pulled the Longstreet book off the nightstand and opened it. I read for a while and then dozed off. When I awoke, my neck was bent backward, and I thought for a moment I was paralyzed from the eyebrows down. It took a bit of effort to get everything back in order. I went into the bathroom and brushed my teeth to take away the deposit that some nasty tooth fairy had left in my mouth while I slept. There could have been no other explanation for how my mouth felt. I finally felt secure enough to go see Leigh.

Leigh and I had lunch at the little Mexican restaurant Tracy and I had visited earlier in the week. It was a place where we went when I had a craving for nachos and marguerites. The nachos were super-hot and the drinks were large and cold. When we entered, the owner, whom I had met at a small poker game one night at a mutual friend's house, steered us to a table in a quiet corner. He pulled out the chair for Leigh and complemented the senorita on a necklace she was wearing.

Although I knew Miguel was from the Texas-Mexico border area and spoke fluent Spanish, I sometimes thought waiters were required to know at least five words in the language of the restaurant in which they worked. Four or five well-pronounced words in almost any language would dissuade me from attempting a conversation.

Leigh spoke Spanish almost as well as Miguel. Every time we went there, I thought they were secretly discussing another place to eat or something equally sinister.

Miguel smiled and left me to wonder.

"We had another car stolen from the parking lot last night," Leigh said. "That's the second one this month." She reached across the table, took my hand, and held it as she spoke. "I think I may not leave my car overnight quite so often. What do you think?"

Before I could answer, Miguel brought two large frosty glasses containing the icy cold Mexican national beverage. We picked up the glasses and touched them together. "To your little red rocket. May a car thief never find it."

The afternoon crowd had cleared out by the time we got there so we had the place almost to ourselves. I sat there for too long without speaking.

"I'm sure glad we're having this little conversation this afternoon." Leigh's voice brought me back to the moment. "Is there something on your mind that we can talk about?" She seldom asked about any of the projects I worked on.

"I'm sorry. I guess I'm running the tapes on Jeff. There are so many pieces of his puzzle that I don't understand."

She squeezed my hand. "You wanna talk through them? You said that helps sometimes. You know, get an outside opinion."

I took a long drink from my glass. "I wouldn't know where to begin. I'm finding a side of the man I would have never thought existed."

"I didn't think you two were such friends."

"We weren't. I might feel the same about almost anyone if I found some of the things I've seen in the last week." I shook my head. "I don't know, Leigh. I may be getting in over my head."

Miguel brought another couple over and seated them at a table near us. They were in their mid-thirties and married. Neither wore a ring but as soon as they were seated, they picked up a menu and, like a wall, they hid behind it from each other. The first words they spoke were to the waiter when he came for their order.

"What have you found that you can talk about?" She hesitated. "I'm assuming Tracy has hired you."

"Yeah, she did." I didn't want to tell Leigh about the photos of Tracy I had found in Jeff's house, but every time I thought of her, that was the image that came to my mind. "She now agrees that there may be more to his death than we know at this time. I promised her I'd look into it." I also failed to mention to either of them my conversation with Marge or my upcoming meeting with her in less than five hours.

# CHAPTER 12

I left my place a little after six. I knew the drive to the east side could take any time from thirty minutes to several hours, depending on traffic. I wanted to give myself plenty of time to get there. From Edmonds to the east side you had only two options, both generally bad choices. I planned to take the 520 Floating Bridge and the extra time would take care of any traffic tie ups along the way. And, besides, I would rather be two hours early than two minutes late. I took the Fifth Avenue through town when I left the office. On its way out of town, Fifth Avenue had about five different names. It alternately became Fifth, Edmonds Way, 205, and a short stretch of it was named in honor of Edmond's Olympic ice skating champion, Rosalyn Sumners. I left it and headed to the interstate.

The east side, as it was known, was where the big money from Microsoft and Boeing lived. It had several sections of houses in walled compounds facing the open waters of Lake Washington. Without looking at the address, I knew the place I was going would be just such a house. Marge had given me directions and instructions, which seemed, at the time, a little strange. The closer I got to the place, the more I needed the directions.

I found the house, or rather the compound, after passing it once. There was a stone and wrought iron fence running parallel to the road for at least three hundred yards. This was not a house that was purchased by someone working for minimum wage. I unfolded the sheet of paper Marge had given me and read the instructions for getting inside once I found the gate.

I pulled my car next to a small box and pushed a white button. I half expected a kid's voice to ask me if I wanted fries with my meal. An adult male voice soon answered my second buzz on the button.

"Yes?"

"My name is Maxwell. I'm a guest of Marge and Barry's."

"Please wait."

I heard the speaker crackle when he spoke. Other than that, the machine was dead.

"I'm going to open the gate for you. Come to the end of the drive and park on the left. Marge will meet you."

The speaker went silent and the gate began to swing open. As I pulled through, I looked to see if I could find a switch to activate the gate from the inside. If it was there, I did not see it. I was driving slowly through the entrance when the gate began to swing back to the closed position. Like it or not, I was committed.

The driveway led to a large house well hidden from the street. It was an old house, in that it had been built back in the fifties when this was still country and the buyer got his money's worth. From the outside, it looked like something seen in photos of Beverly Hills or other moneyed neighborhoods. There were a dozen or so cars along the driveway. They ranged from a Jag to my Toyota. I saw a white Buick that I thought Marge had parked in front of my office earlier in the week. There was a space beside it so I pulled into the vacancy.

Marge was standing beside my door before I cut the engine and unbuckled the seat belt. I exited, and together we walked up the driveway toward the house.

"I'm glad you came. You're gonna find this to be most interesting." I felt her reach down and take my hand. As we approached the house, I caught a glimpse of a number of other people through a waist-high hedge of small bushes. They were standing around on what I assumed to be a poolside patio. I could hear water splashing, and a slow easy jazz tune was playing over speakers mounted overhead. At the end of the pool, I saw steam rising from an in-ground hot tub or Jacuzzi. The rich smell of someone cooking over an open fire filled my head.

"The first person I want to introduce you to is my husband, Barry. We'll find him by the bar." Her voice brought me back to the present as I continued to look around.

Marge dropped my hand, took my arm, and steered me gently toward an opening to the house from the patio. Before we got there, we were approached by a woman headed toward the activity outside. I knew my movements were anything but subtle as I watched the woman. She wore a very short beach jacket of some type. It was tied loosely around her. Even so, I could tell she was completely nude beneath it. I tried to divert my eyes and was reasonable successful until Marge stopped her.

"Ellie, this is my guest, Max. He's going to spend some time with us tonight."

Ellie extended her hand but Marge stopped her. "Not so fast. I said he was my guest." They both laughed at something I obviously did not quite understand.

The action of Ellie's attempt to shake hands had caused her robe to slip completely open. My earlier suspicions were confirmed. She was as naked as the day she entered this earth. "Okay. But I'll see you later, Max." Ellie laughed and strode toward the patio without adjusting her robe.

I looked behind us to the pool and, as I did, I saw an equally nude man climb from the water and take a towel to wrap around himself. I felt Marge tug at my arm as she tried to guide me inside.

I held back. "I think we need to talk." I said, "Give me the twenty second version of what's going on here."

"Let's go in the television room. I think you'll find it a little saner. We can talk in there." Without waiting, she led me through the kitchen to a small room where a very large screen television was playing. We were the only people in the room.

"This is the end of the conversation I started in your office last week. I told you that you'd find the Final Frontier to be one extreme or another." She opened a small silver box on an end table and took out a cigarette. From the same box, she produced a wooden match, which she struck against the side of the box. She took a deep drag, held the smoke, and let it go. I didn't have to ask to know she didn't buy those at the local Seven/Eleven.

"This place is known as a party house. All of the people here think of themselves as very liberated in their thinking and in their attitudes."

"And in their dress codes."

"Why, Mister Maxwell, we're not a little prudish, are we?"

"No, I think I'm just a little off guard, that's all."

She took another long drag from her smoke. "I thought about telling you but I decided it was best to let you see what this place is all about." She hesitated. "Then you'd know why I said what I did about my husband and Jeff."

For the first time since arriving, Marge seemed to

slip from a shock effect mode to the person whom I had first spoken to.

I motioned toward the couch. This time, I led her. "Let's sit. You still owe me the twenty second version."

The twenty-second version took almost fifteen minutes. In that time, Marge told me a story I would never have believed, especially in little Edmonds. It may have been more palatable anywhere else in the world but not here. Outside in the pool and in a variety of rooms throughout the house were some of the most prominent citizens of Seattle and its environs. Most were with their spouse or significant other. A very few were alone. That was a temporary condition and one frowned upon by the rest of the members, especially if the guest were male. They came from a wide variety of backgrounds. There was a banker and his wife, a plastic surgeon and her boyfriend, several white-collar executives, at least one auto mechanic, and some who wished to retain their anonymity. The one thing they all had in common was their desire to participate with, or watch, other couples as they had sex.

The membership was controlled and each member had to undergo a blood test every six months. Marge explained the rules of admission and participation. What she didn't tell me was the why. She was about to when the door opened and a man walked into the room.

She saw him and immediately got up from the couch. She looked first at him and then at me. "Max, I'd like you to meet my husband, Barry." She turned toward him. "Barry, this is Max."

Barry was like everyone else I met that evening. He was from middle America. Normally he would not have stood out in any crowd but there was something vaguely familiar about him. He was in his late thirties, stood about six one, had slightly graying dark hair, and a pronounced beer belly. He came across the room and stood directly in front of me. The closer he got, the more I felt like I knew him.

"Max. It's good to meet you." He immediately started looking around the room.

I didn't know what he was looking for but Marge did. "Max is alone tonight."

Barry laughed. "Well, don't let it worry you, Max. It won't last long around here." He turned to Marge. "Could I see you for a minute?"

I didn't know if I should excuse myself and go back outside or if they were leaving. With the place being so open in every other way, I thought it rather strange a man would want to tell his wife something in secret. Secrets were a commodity that I felt were in short supply at the Final Frontier.

"Max, if you'll wait here a minute, I be right back. I can show you the rest of the Frontier," Marge said as she and Barry left the room.

There was one window in the room. It was on a wall facing the open grounds of the compound. I saw several large trees between the house and the road. If there was a better place for a club of this type in the area, I wasn't aware of where it could be placed. My guess was that the place covered from four to six acres. It appeared to be enclosed on all sides, as I could see a fence on the north and east sides of the land. I had passed the southern fence and the one along the road coming in. From the window, I could also see the driveway. I watched two more cars enter. One was a small sports car of some sort and the other was a bright red Cherokee. A man and woman got out of each. Both couples seemed to know each other as they made their way up the driveway toward the house. I was still watching the road when Marge came back into the room.

"Sorry. He wanted to—"

I held up my hand to stop her. "I may not want to know what he wanted."

"You're right." She hesitated then took another perfectly rolled joint from the silver box. "I hope you don't mind." She lit the piece and walked to the window. "I never needed anything to pick me up or bring me down when I came here before. But I seem to need all the help I can get tonight."

I felt like I was caught in some sort of a vortex. I was spinning around, not knowing where I was going but not getting anywhere either. I did not like the feeling, and I wanted to get in or get out. "Marge, when we spoke in my office, you led me to believe you had some information that was related to the death of Jeff Payton. If memory serves me, you even said you thought you knew who did it and why. If you don't mind, I'd kinda like to start the conversation where we left off."

"What if I told you that, at this very moment, there are almost one hundred people around us who are having sex? Some of them are with the person they brought with them, but a great majority are with someone else. Some are watching, some are participating. There are couples, threesomes, foursomes, and what you would call orgies going on in almost every room in this house." She walked to the window and watched as another car parked. "The rules are simple. Do whatever you want to here and, when you leave, you go back to being the nice young couple next door until the next time you meet. That's how it's supposed to work. Most of the time, it does."

"And other times?"

"Contrary to what you may think, all of us here are humans. And we don't always play by the rules." She walked to a liquor cabinet and opened it. I watched as she poured herself a healthy scotch with a tiny splash of water. "If you want anything, I'm sure it's in there." She played with her drink for a moment then walked to the doorway leading back to the rest of the house. "Let's get out of here. We can talk while I show you around."

Without waiting for me, she opened the door. Once again, Marge took my arm. We could have been friends or lovers strolling in the park on a Sunday afternoon. "I don't know how much you know about this lifestyle," she said, "but I'll assume it's not very much, and I'll start with the basics."

"That probably would be helpful," I said as we approached the pool. I saw Ellie again. I hardly recognized her since all I was able to see was her face as she was caught in the obvious throes of passion with the man who lay atop her at poolside.

"Everyone here is in what we like to refer to as 'An Alternative Lifestyle.' Some people call us wife swappers or swingers, but those terms are pretty much passé now."

We walked by Ellie and her partner. Marge hardly looked down when we passed.

"I'm glad you told me. I'd hate to get the terminology wrong."

"We're very selective about who we allow in here. For obvious reasons. One of our first rules is we try to find people who won't be judgmental till they know the whole story."

Although she didn't say so, I knew she wanted me to hold my comments till she finished.

"In the lifestyle, you can have a closed swing and an open swing. This is an open swing." She guided me toward the hot tub.

"Okay, what's the difference?"

"Good question. In an open swing, you can participate or not. It's the call of the individual."

"And in a closed?"

"In a closed swing, anything and everything goes. If someone wants you to join or wants to join you—"

"I get the picture." In the hot tub, a woman sat in a man's lap. She was facing him. I didn't think they were discussing the weather.

"Barry and I joined about three years ago. We've met a lot of very nice people here. We've even become friends with some of them outside the club."

As soon as she said that, I knew where I had met Barry before. Although I hadn't actually met him, I had seen his picture. I was certain he was the person in the photos with Tracy Payton. I stopped walking. "Is that where Jeff and Tracy come in?"

Marge was looking toward the wooded area beyond the house. She spoke without looking at me. "We met them on line about a year ago."

"On line?" I asked, thinking I already knew the answer.

"Yes. We first met them through a computer chat room. We talked for about a month and then found out we both lived in the Seattle area. We set up a meeting and liked what we saw." She stopped to check out my reaction. When I didn't say or do anything she found disagreeable, she continued. "After meeting and going on a couple of trips together, they introduced us to this place. They were here for the same reasons as everyone else. The spark had left their marriage. They didn't want to destroy the security they had by getting caught having an affair and risking a messy divorce. So they came here."

Marge opened a small bag she carried and extracted another joint. Her face took on a soft glow as she touched a match to the end.

She took two quick hits then continued. "Barry and Jeff had a lot in common, at least sexually. I know you've heard it said about a man that he'd fuck a snake if somebody would hold the snake's head. That's Barry. Jeff, on the other hand, took it a step further. He'd stick his dick under a rock on the off chance there was a snake beneath it. He simply couldn't get enough sex."

"And Tracy? Where did she fit into the picture?" I thought of the irony of my statement after I'd made it.

"On a scale of one to ten, her sex drive is about a seven point five." She took a long drag, held it, and spoke in the smoky voice one gets when exhaling and speaking at the same time. "Mine is half a point better. I'm a solid eight. Just in case you wondered."

I heard a woman begin to moan from the vicinity of the hot tub. It was quickly followed by a male sound not unlike a bull elk in rutting season.

"The one rule you never break is to have an affair with one of the people from the club, on the side, without your mate knowing."

"Sounds to me like you're about to tell me you broke that rule." The sounds were coming to a crescendo behind us.

"I did."

"With Jeff?"

"About six months ago we, Jeff and I, started to meet for lunch once or twice a week. By the end of the month, we were skipping lunch and going straight to a local motel. Barry followed me one day and caught us."

I looked around at the surroundings and wondered why someone would feel a need to go to a motel if this was waiting for them. "I take it he played the part of the jealous husband?"

"Unbelievably so. I found it hard to understand at first."

"At first?"

"Even if you don't approve of what we're doing here, Max, we do have rules. I broke the most basic one.

We came here to keep from cheating on each other, and I broke that rule."

"What was Barry's response?"

"He told Jeff he was going to kill him."

"Do you think he would carry out the threat? Is Barry capable of killing someone? It's one thing to make a threat. It's an entirely different matter to actually carry it out."

"He has an uncontrollable temper. You wouldn't think it to look at him, but it's there. I've seen it. I've even been on the receiving end of it a couple of times." She let her eyes look at the ground instead of me. Her family secret was a violent relationship. I looked around us and wondered about the standards we used to judge each other.

"Okay, let's say for the purpose of this conversation, I believe Barry could have done it. We've established motive. I'm afraid that's not enough. He has to have opportunity and knowledge of how to commit the crime."

Another couple came by us as we stood there. The man was in his early thirties. The woman looked like she was barely out of her training bra.

Marge saw my reaction as they passed. "Just so you don't think too badly of us, she's twenty-two. She's a model for teenage clothes."

"Thanks. I think." I steered her back toward the house. "Jeff died in a diving accident. Does Barry dive?"

"The four of us went to Mexico for a week when we first met."

"Do you know where he was the day Jeff died?"

"That's the best or worst part. I've asked him and he refused to tell me."

As we walked, we neared the open pit where a man was cooking steaks and ribs. Each steak was at least a pound of meat. Large metal bowls of baked beans and stacks of baked potatoes and corn on the cob lined the edge of the grill. Of all the possible temptations I'd seen since I arrived at the Final Frontier, this was the biggest.

With very little urging from Marge, we filled a plate and took a seat at the far end of the pool. After I took my seat, Marge excused herself to go get us something to drink. For the second time since I arrived, I was alone. Again, it didn't last long.

I barely heard the voice from my deaf side. "So, how do you like our little club?" I quickly turned and saw Barry and another woman standing behind me. Both were wearing terry cloth robes, not unlike you'd find in a good hotel or a spa. Barry's was long. Hers was not. Neither had the robe tied in the front. It was not something I needed to see while I was trying to have dinner. I felt like I was stage side at a co-ed strip show.

"This is Max's first time," Barry said as he watched my reaction.

"First time here or at a party house?" The woman had a slight German accent.

"Yes." I was still sitting and I momentarily wondered what Miss Manners would say about the protocol. Did one stand for a naked lady or continue to sit? I was saved from the decision by Marge, who returned with two draft mugs of beer. As soon as she got close to the table, Barry and his lady friend left.

She watched them disappear into the crowd gathered around the hot tub. "Looks like Barry found somebody to help him through the grief of losing his friend."

I tried to make polite conversation. "Does she come here often?"

"No. She's from one of the Portland clubs. They do things a little bit differently down there."

That was a fairly scary thought.

# CHAPTER 13

It was almost two a.m. when I left the Final Frontier and drove home. About half the cars were already gone. The other half belonged to people who were staying for the weekend. Many of those were still in or around the pool and hot tub when Marge walked me to my Toyota. By that time, I had seen Barry on two other occasions. Each time, he was with a different woman. I spent the last hour with Marge telling me about how she and Barry and Jeff and Tracy had become regulars at the party house and how they had taken their mutual friendship and desires beyond the gates of the compound.

Although I hadn't mentioned finding the photos, she told me about several trips they made together and how they had gotten into photography. For her, it was like talking about a ski trip to Aspen.

Several times when I was overseas in the army, I had seen live sex shows. They were always in some back-alley club. The participants, for the most part, were prostitutes who were too old or too ugly for even a drunk, horny GI to take on. The shows were accompanied by the yells of encouragement from an audience who was generally too drunk to do anything other than shout.

There, it was a business done for money. What I witnessed earlier in the evening was anything but a business.

When I got back to my place, I was too keyed up to sleep so I picked out a movie from the stack I had recorded from the premium channels and put it in the DVD player. Although I subscribed to the service, I hardly ever watched a movie when it was shown on the television. I usually recorded them for occasions such as this one. I selected one that had been a blockbuster at the theaters. I had also missed it there.

With the film running and the sound where it was more to block out the constant ringing in my ear than anything else, I lay down on the bed without taking off more than my shoes.

Marge's explanation of why they participated in the club was still whirling through my head when I was finally over taken by sleep. Two thoughts kept competing with her for attention, though. One was Barry. I felt after meeting him that he was capable of doing everything Marge wanted to believe about him. The other thought was Leigh. I felt incredibly close to her. I wanted to see her or hear her voice. I even picked up the phone and was about to hit the speed dial for her number when I stopped. She had worked all evening. Why awaken her at this hour? I would see her later in the morning.

I heard the noise but I couldn't find it. At first, I thought it was my alarm clock. When my eyes opened sufficiently to focus, I saw it was turned off. It had to be the phone.

I reached for the handset and, with some effort, placed it against my ear when I finally found it.

"Hello?" My voice cracked, as if I was going through a second puberty. I cleared my throat and tried again. "Hello."

"It's a beautiful day and you're still in bed. Where's that old army spirit. Up at four, run five miles, and then go out and wage war on innocent women and children! Rape, pillage, and plunder! God, I miss it."

"I'm sorry. You've obviously got the wrong number. This is the monastery. We're all monks here." I looked at the clock. It was blinking eight-fifty-one and my brother-in-law was on the phone. "What the hell do you want, Harry?"

"Is that any way to talk to the one in-law you have who'll still speak to you?" Harry, also now a military retiree, had met my sister when she visited me at Fort Hood, Texas. They started writing and when he went to the University of Georgia for his Masters, they started dating and got married.

"I thought I'd grace you with an appearance and let you take me skiing. The rest of the mob is going to Georgia to visit your mother. I figured taking a chance on a broken leg was the lesser of the two evils."

I heard his smoker's cough hacking in the background. "When are you coming?"

I was fully awake and moving into the kitchen for a cup of left-over coffee. He gave me his travel plans, and I agreed to make the reservations for us to stay at a ski lodge near Snoqualmie Pass. It was late enough in the year that we would probably have to go to Canada to find snow. Neither of us was an accomplished skier but we did have a good time when he made his annual visit.

I finished talking to him and my sister and was sitting on the couch, still in my boxer shorts reading the newspaper, when I heard a key slide into the lock on my front door.

I had no reason to believe it was anything or anyone except Leigh, however, with the actions of the last few days, I didn't want to take any unnecessary chances. I left the table and slipped quietly back to my bedroom where I pulled a pistol from the drawer beside my bed. I stood, pistol in hand, and watched the door slowly open.

I heard Leigh before I saw her enter. She must have thought I was still asleep. She quietly removed her jacket and laid it across the back of the couch. I back-peddled to the bedroom placed the gun back in the drawer, and slipped beneath the covers on the bed.

It was not unusual for her to come by on Sunday when we did not spend the night together. Several times, I had been awakened with her attempting to slip quietly into bed with me. We both knew I was such a light sleeper that it would be virtually impossible to do it, but it never stopped her from trying. As usual, I faked sleep until neither of us could stand it any longer.

This time, there was no faking on either of our parts.

We made love listening to the sounds of a Sunday morning jazz program on the radio.

We had a late brunch at a place on the water by the locks in Ballard. It was once a restaurant with a varied menu and a bartender who took pride in his work. It had changed hands, without my knowing, and now featured an Italian cuisine. I was disappointed and finally ordered something from the menu I didn't like and could hardly eat. I would have left if I had been alone, but Leigh was too sensitive to the feelings of restaurant workers to upset them.

It started raining about an hour after we finished eating so we went back to my place, curled up on the couch, and started to read what was left of the paper. Midway through a bottle of wine, we forgot about the paper. As we made love, I thought about the couples I had seen the night before and wondered who they were with just then.

I was lying quietly with Leigh curled up beside me. She rose up on one elbow. "Tell me about last night."

"What about it?" I was caught a little off guard that she would even ask.

"You hardly ever work late like that. I just wondered what you did."

I turned to face her. "You wouldn't believe me if I told you."

"Try me," she touted.

I spent the next hour telling her about the previous evening at the Final Frontier. When I finished, she surprised me by asking if I planned to go back.

"I don't think I'll have to. Why?"

"Oh, I don't know. I just thought if you did, I'd better go with you."

I saw part of Leigh that I had not seen before. "Would you be going for my benefit or for yours?"

Leigh sat up in the bed. The sheet slipped, baring her breast. She slowly pulled it back in place. "A little of both. I knew a couple who were into wife swapping about ten years ago. They even approached Frank and me about joining them."

"I can't believe you. Here I am, out half the night with a bunch of people who're screwing everything and everybody in sight, and you're telling me you know all about it." I really felt like I'd been born in the last century. "I guess the army sheltered its families from more than we realized."

"I'm certain it goes on in every walk of life. It's probably not as well organized as what you saw, but it's there." She hesitated then shrugged. "The main issue is, did you get what you went after, no pun intended?"

I told her about Marge's visit to my office and her suspicions of her husband having killed Jeff.

"Do you think he did?"

"What I think is that I'm getting in over my head. If Jeff was killed and Barry was responsible, it's a matter for the police, not for me." I got out of bed and went to the dresser where I had a small envelope. "Here, I want you to see these." I handed her the photos I picked up when I went through Jeff's boxes.

She examined each one carefully. "I assume, from what you've told me that the other couple is Marge and Barry."

"In the flesh!"

I was about to put the photos back in the envelope when the phone rang. I picked up the one by the bed and answered it.

"Hello." There was no voice on the other end. "Hello, hello? If you're there, speak up. If this is a game, I don't want to play."

I was about to break the connection when I heard the male voice. It sounded like the person was covering the mouthpiece with a handkerchief or cupping his hand over it to distort his voice or make it deeper.

"Why can't you let well enough alone?"

"It's a character flaw of mine. I've had to live with it all these years. What should I leave alone?" I motioned for Leigh to hand me the tape recorder I kept in my closet. I wanted to see if I could record the voice on the other end.

"You know what I'm talking about. Jeff Payton's death is none of your business. You could fuck around with it and get yourself hurt."

"Hurt? Like how?" Leigh handed me the recorder and I hooked the microphone over the phone. If it worked I'd at least have a copy of the conversation.

"Yeah hurt, like—"

"Like Jeff got hurt?" The cassette was running. I wouldn't know until I replayed it if I had anything.

"Exactly. The same thing could happen to you."

With that comment, I moved Jeff's death from accidental to very suspicious bordering on murder one. "I'd really like to talk to you. Why don't we meet—"

"We've already met, sort of. I don't think you'd like to meet me again," he quickly replied.

"Let me guess. You think shooting up my house from the street is supposed to get my attention, right?" I didn't want to admit it but it was quite effective.

The look of horror on Leigh's face reminded me that I had failed to mention the incident to her.

"Nobody wants you messing around in something that doesn't concern you. Leave us and Coach Payton alone."

I heard him hang up the receiver and the line began to buzz. I placed my phone back on its cradle.

"What the hell was that all about?" Leigh was out of bed and dressing as she talked. "And what's this about somebody shooting at you? You didn't say anything—"

I quickly took her in my arms in an attempt to calm her down or at least stop her from talking long enough to explain.

She accepted everything as part of an investigation until I got to the part about having my apartment shot up. "I can't believe somebody fired shots into your apartment and you didn't even try to press charges. This is not Baghdad! You're not in combat. People don't do things like that and get away with it."

I started to tell her more people got caught and punished in a war zone far more frequently that they did in any big city on Saturday night. Somehow, I didn't think she'd understand the irony of what I was trying to say. "I did report it and Gunny came by. We thought it was just a car load of kids and I didn't take it personally."

"Do you now?"

She stood with her hands on her hips. If I didn't give the right answer, it would be like waving a red flag in front of a bull.

"Very much so." My assurance calmed her a bit. "So

much that the first thing I'm gonna do tomorrow is go see Gunny and tell him what I've found out."

"You do that and then call me." She was so upset that she left without another word.

I went by my office early on Monday morning. When I got there, I had two calls on my machine and an envelope that someone other than the mailman had dropped through the mail slot. I picked up the envelope and took it to my desk where I pulled out a long letter opener and slipped it beneath the flap. In one long slice, I had the envelope open and its contents on my desk. It was a letter, not unlike the ransom notes we saw in the movies.

Someone had cut letters and words from magazines and newspapers. I stared at the words: *He was an evil person. Justice has prevailed. He won't hurt anyone again.* Some were complete words while others had been formed and misspelled a letter at a time. I carefully placed the letter and the envelope in a larger one and laid it on my desk. It would be difficult to make something like that and not leave a fingerprint.

I activated my answering machine and got the first message. It was from Mister Tice. He wanted me to meet him to discuss how I was doing in my investigation of the thieves in his store. A nagging feeling told me I would earn all the money he paid me. The second call was a very pleasant voice telling me about her diving trip to the San Juan Islands and asking me to call her on Monday. Anna like Madonna and not Anna like banana had a way of making her voice sound like the words were mixed with twenty-year-old scotch.

On the way to the office, I stopped by the bakery and picked up a muffin and large coffee. I opened the bag and took the two items out. I was putting sugar in my coffee when the phone rang.

It got to the second ring before I reached it. "Maxwell here. May I help you?"

"You really do keep early hours." It was Tracy. "I talked to Marge yesterday. I think you and I probably need to talk. Can you meet me later this morning? I start working at the school again tomorrow."

I told her I had to meet Mister Tice and I could see her any time after eleven. She agreed with my suggestion to come to my office. I placed two more calls and sat down at my desk to eat my breakfast.

# Chapter 14

I arrived at the mall a little after nine. The stores were not yet open but the mall was filled with people who used it as an indoor walking track. Most of the walkers were elderly people who seemed to make it more of a social event than an hour of exercise. I fell in behind one man who must have been in his late seventies. He walked the circle as briskly as anyone there. I wanted to get a feel of what or who was in the mall early in the morning and who might be using that time to clean out the gift shop.

I walked pass the shop once as I went with the walkers then I went to a bench not far from the shop and sat down. I took more than a few stares and looks of pity from the people much older than me who were still up walking. One little lady stopped and offered to walk with me. The embarrassment got to me after ten minutes so I moved on.

At a quarter of ten, I was still walking. I saw Mister Tice when he entered the shop. There were already two other employees in there when he tapped on the door for them to turn off the alarm so he could enter. As soon as he was inside, I saw one of the two employees leave the shop and head toward the food court.

I followed when she took a second turn and went

outside to the parking lot. With hardly a glance back, she headed straight to her car. She opened the trunk and placed a small bag she had beneath her jacket in the trunk. I copied down her tag number and followed her back into the mall.

As soon as I got inside, I called Mister Tice. I had to wait for the clerk who answered to get him.

"This is Bob Tice may I help you?"

"This is Maxwell. I may have an idea about your losses. What time did you get to the shop today?"

"I came in a little early. I got here about nine forty five. I hadn't planned to come by the mall location until after eleven. I was going by the shop in downtown Seattle first. Why?"

His coming early explained the woman taking the stuff out when he was in the shop. She probably had it packed and ready to go. When he came in, it disrupted her time schedule so she had to get it out immediately. "I saw something this morning I want to follow up on. I'll probably see you tomorrow. Will you be there or at one of the other shops?"

"I'm coming by here for the first half of the day."

"Does anyone else know what your schedule is?"

"No, I haven't told—"

I quickly interrupted. "Tell your employees you'll be somewhere else tomorrow. Then I want you to come in just like you did today. Same time, same everything. Will the same employees be working tomorrow?"

I heard him flip through several sheets of paper that I assumed was a schedule.

"Yes, the same ones."

"Okay, that's good. Just tell them you'll not be in until late tomorrow and then show up just like you did today. Once you're in the shop, it's business as usual for you. Don't do or say anything out of the ordinary. I'll call you tomorrow if I have anything." I ended the conversation before he could ask too many questions.

When I left the mall, it was time to drive back to my office to meet Tracy.

There was some construction on one of the main arteries leading to and from the shopping mall, so I had to take a short detour. I always wondered why road construction had to take place in daylight hours. It would seem to me the best time to do it was from about seven in the evening until five or six the next morning. That would make about as much sense as selecting the contractor by who gave a guarantee on their work and not on the basis of the low bidder.

When I arrived at the office, I saw Tracy's car parked on the street in front of the building. Since the city only gave out parking tickets on Wednesdays, she was safe. She could park as long as she needed.

I drove around the building and parked in my space. As I emerged from the parking lot, she saw me and got out of her car.

"Been waiting long?" I asked as I singled out the key to my office door from my key ring.

"Only a minute or so. Actually, I was listening to a song on the radio. I wanted to finish it before I came in." She unconsciously bit her lip. "It was a favorite of Jeff's."

I unlocked the door and stepped aside for her to enter. She went to the couch and had a seat. She wore a pair of dark blue pants and a lighter blue blouse of a very soft silky-looking material. I was sure if she took the blouse off and did not immediately hang it, she would have no more than a handful of fabric weighing less than if it was cotton candy. She had her hair in a small ponytail.

"I'll save you the possible embarrassment of broaching the subject first. When we first met in here, I told you there were some things about Jeff and me that you might not understand. Remember?"

I nodded."

"One of them is, or was, the Final Frontier, although I'm sure you have a better understanding of that since you went there on Saturday." Tracy looked out toward the street as she spoke.

I felt I needed to get to the heart of the situation I had been hired for. "Look, Tracy, you hired me because we felt there might be more to Jeff's death than we knew. For what it's worth, that doesn't includes me either condoning or condemning any lifestyle you and Jeff might have lived."

I noticed the red light was flashing on my answering machine. I had two messages. They would have to wait.

"Looks like I made the right choice when I hired you, Max." Tracy stood and picked up her purse. She pulled her checkbook from inside it and opened the folder over the checks. "I want to hire you to find out if Jeff's death was more than an accident as reported by the police. What is your normal rate and how much should I give you as a retainer?" Her demeanor changed to one of seriousness.

I accepted the fact that, if I was going to do this, I needed to do it right. I told her my rate and she wrote a check for ten days services.

"I need to ask you some questions, Tracy, so please sit back down." I wanted the conversation to be somewhere between the two extremes she had shown in the last five minutes. "Do you know of anyone who would want to kill Jeff?"

She was quiet for too long. "There's only one I can think of."

"Barry?"

"Marge told you about the four of us?"

"She did. And she also mentioned that she was seeing Jeff on the side. Breaking one of the rules was how she described it. Did you know about that?"

"I didn't at first. Then I found a receipt for a motel where they spent an afternoon. I'm not certain but I think Jeff wanted me to find it."

"What makes you think that?"

"I never went through his pants pockets. It was not something I did. One night, he asked me to hand him everything in his pockets while he was changing clothes. The receipt was there and he had to know it."

"Was it a hostile confrontation?"

Tracy laughed before she answered. "That's a good observation. Two couples exchange mates with everyone's knowledge and approval. Then my husband has an affair with the wife of the man I was sleeping with and I get upset. I guess it doesn't make a hell of a lot of sense to you, does it?"

"I'm trying to understand."

She laughed again. "I guess you'd have to be there."

I walked to the back room and flipped the switch on my coffee maker. I had put it together earlier, and all I had to do was wait for it to brew. "Was there enough anger to cause Barry to want to kill Jeff?" I asked as I returned to the main room.

"Jeff knew Barry was upset with him, but he didn't think it would last or that it was very serious."

"Jeff told you that?" I opened the drawer, got out a yellow legal pad, and began to make notes.

"Jeff told me he and Barry could patch things up. I think they planned to meet and talk the week Jeff died."

I could smell the coffee from the back room. "Was Barry capable of murder? Do you think he could deliberately plan and carry out the killing of another human being, especially one that was his friend?" Without waiting for an answer, I went in back and poured two mugs of coffee. I brought one and placed it beside Tracy.

"You have to understand the relationship between the four of us." She sipped at the coffee. "Let me finish, I know you don't want to hear some of this but I think it's essential."

For the next thirty minutes Tracy spun a tale that one would expect to find in the letters section of a men's magazine. They had attended a national convention of like-minded couples in Las Vegas the previous summer. She told me how they were all supposed to remain faithful to their own little groups, and how they got their regular blood tests. This was a group of prominent citizens of the community enjoying sex at its lowest common denominator. At times, she got very specific with what and how they did the various things, where they did them, and with whom.

I tried to keep it in a professional mode but after having seen the photos of Tracy, it was difficult. There was no denying she was a very attractive woman.

By the time she stopped talking, I was convinced Barry was still a prime suspect in the death of Jeff Payton.

We were interrupted by a phone call. I let it go and my machine picked it up. I ignored it and gave my full attention to Tracy.

She glanced down at her watch. "It's almost one. Do you have any plans for lunch?" She stood. "Since you're on my payroll and I'm covering expenses, I may as well spring for lunch." She glanced toward the desk and saw the red light blinking. "Why don't you give me a few minutes' head start and meet me at the Waterfront Cafe. I'll go and get us a table." Without waiting for a reply, she left the office.

As soon as she left the office, I pushed the button to

listen to my messages. They were both from the same person. It was a man who left a number and asked me to get back to him as soon as possible. I got a lot of calls like that so I didn't pay a lot of attention to the first one. It was his second call that got me to respond.

I dialed the number he gave me. A man on the third ring answered it. "Mister Getz, please. This is Maxwell returning his call."

"This is Getz. Thanks for calling back."

I didn't want to go through a bunch of pleasantries. "In your call you said this had something to do with the death of Jeff Payton."

"That's right. I represent his insurance company. It seems Mister Payton had a fairly substantial amount of insurance—"

He didn't have to finish. If Jeff's death was accidental, they owed double. Although it would surely be accidental, at least for Jeff, any way it happened, they needed to know. Insurance companies were quite often more diligent and thorough in their investigations than the police. The police did it for statistics. The insurance company was money motivated.

"I'm already under a contract. I have a client, Mister Getz."

"Oh, I'm certain you do, Mister Maxwell. I want you to know we will be offering a substantial payment to the person who can give us information that leads to the conviction of any party responsible for Mister Payton's death."

"You have a copy of the ME's report. It says death by drowning." I hesitated, to see if he would say anything. He didn't. "Do you think there's something more to it, Mister Getz?"

"We'd like to know what you think, Mister Maxwell. Can we meet somewhere tomorrow?"

I felt the ball bounce back into my court. "How about my office at three tomorrow?"

"Fine, I'll be there." He hung up and the line began to buzz.

I knew from other talks with insurance investigators what he wanted and why. If Jeff's death was suicide, they did not have to pay on the double indemnity clause. If it was murder, it was still considered an accident, and they paid double. I was certain Jeff would feel that way. The catch was if it was murder and the policy beneficiary was involved, they could hold up payment for years while the lawyers went through a series of very-time-consuming appeals. They didn't have to pay, the stockholders made money off the funds they didn't pay out, and whoever proved it got a finder's fee. That was where he wanted to use my services.

I left the office and drove down Main toward the ferry dock and the Waterfront Cafe. On the way, I thought of the things Tracy had said in my office. She had given me a thorough picture of her late husband and their relationship. The one piece she had left out was anything dealing with school and the activities I kept hearing about in Portland. I knew that was a big piece of the puzzle and, if I was going to be expected to put it together, I needed those pieces.

Just as I crossed the railroad tracks and turned left on Sunset, a car sped past me going in the opposite direction. I had to stop my turn to keep from being hit by the car as it peeled out of a parking lot and on to the street. It was a fading image in my rearview mirror when it hit me that I might have seen the car before. I strained to get a look but, by then, it had disappeared up the hill and into the city. All I could say for certain was the car was a small sports variety like a Camaro or Firebird and it had a single male driver. I tried to get the tag number but it was reversed in my mirror and the car was too far away.

I found a parking place on the street in front of the Waterfront. I saw Tracy's car in the lot across the street. When I walked through the open front door, I immediately spotted Tracy at a booth in the far corner. There was a woman talking to her so I slowed my pace to give them time to finish their conversation. I pulled a quarter from my pocket and stuck it in the pull-tab machine. As usual, I came up a loser. Just as I threw the losing ticket away, I saw the woman lean down and give Tracy a slight peck on the cheek. She smiled and the woman left.

I slid in the booth across from Tracy. "I didn't keep you waiting. Did I?"

"No. I was just talking to a woman whose son Jeff coached last year." She stared across the table to the open window behind me. "It's amazing how many lives a school teacher touches. Sometimes even we don't realize it." She picked up a glass of water and took a sip. "I can tell you the names of every teacher I ever had from grammar school through high school graduation. I'll bet you could too if you thought about it."

I thought she had given me the opportunity I needed. "You haven't told me much about Jeff's work at school. Exactly what did he do?" Before she could answer a waitress came to take our order. Tracy ordered a bowl of clam chowder and a small salad. I got a BLT.

"As you know, he was the football coach for a number of years. He was also one of the counselors for the senior girls. His main subject was American history, although he taught social studies for two years. That was about five years ago. Since then he's been devoting more time to the counseling and football."

"How many of the seniors did he work with? Was it only with the young ladies?" I thought I already knew the answer to that one.

"Yes. His counseling session were with the senior girls. We wanted to find a female to do it but he had a background that was conducive to his role. He did mostly career counseling. How to find a college they could afford or where to get money if they couldn't afford to pay."

"What about alternatives?"

At the sound of the word she smiled then it quickly faded. "He'd steer them to a trade or job if that's what they wanted."

The waitress brought our food. Tracy loaded her chowder with pepper till the top was almost black.

"Is it unusual for the girls to have a male counselor?" I took a bite from my sandwich.

"Maybe in the old days, but not now. He had a double master's. One of them was in counseling. He, nor the school, saw anything wrong with it." She hesitated as she was about to take a spoonful of chowder. "And neither did I."

"Did Jeff ever have business that took him out of town?"

"You mean other than football games? I can't think of any. He liked dog and horse racing so he went to the track in Portland when they were running."

"Did you go with him?" It was the first time she had given me a reason for his being in Portland.

"I tried it a couple of times but it bored me to tears. You stand around for twenty minutes between races of sixty seconds. That's one pleasure I'll leave to someone else."

She told me about some of the vacations they took but was careful to tell me she always accompanied him. She even mentioned one trip they took with Marge and Barry. We continued to make small and polite conversation as the place filled with the lunch crowd.

Tracy and I finished our lunch and I walked her to the door where we went our separate ways. I watched as she got in her car and drove up the hill through the center of town and back toward her house. As soon as she was out of sight, I got into my Toyota and headed to the police station. I wanted to talk to Gunny again.

I called Gunny's number from my truck. The dispatcher said he was on patrol so she took my number and said she'd give it to him. I didn't want to get involved in anything until I spoke to him so I drove up to Aurora Avenue and took my truck through the car wash. I had the deluxe version so the man was still using the vacuum on the floors when my cell phone began to ring.

"Colonel, Gunny here. What can I do for you?"

"I'd like to buy you a cup if you've got a minute. I've got something for you."

"Where are you now?"

"I'm at the car wash on Aurora. Tell me where to meet you. and I'll come to you." I had to motion for the man to turn off his vacuum hose. It was drowning out Gunny so badly I could hardly hear him.

"There's a pancake joint about two blocks north. I'll be there in ten minutes. I'm running a solo patrol today." He added the last part in case I had something I did not want to say in front of anyone except him.

When I retired from the army, I seriously thought about going to work for a small town police force. I gave up on the idea when I realized how much coffee I would have to drink. The coffee consumption of a police officer was exceeded only by that of a soldier.

I was at a booth when Gunny entered. He saw me and pointed to the men's room where he immediately headed.

A few minutes later, he pulled his nightstick from his belt, placed it on the seat, then slid in beside it. I already had an insulated pot of coffee on the table so I poured him a cup.

"Thanks. I was headed here anyway. I was ready for a pit stop."

I didn't want to take more time than he was willing to give, so I got to the point. "You know I've been hired to look into Jeff Payton's death." He nodded. "I'm beginning to think there may be more to it than was originally thought."

Gunny looked up at me. "Are we on or off the record?"

"Right now we're still off. I just need you to fill in a couple of blanks for me."

"And?"

"And I'll do the same for you." I knew from past conversations Gunny had no desire to become a detective but a high-profile case like Jeff's, if there was more to it, would have another set of rewards just as important to his uniformed career.

"What do you need?"

"First, I may have seen our shooter from last week in town today. At least the car fit the description."

"Did they try something again?"

"No, I passed it on the way to lunch. He came out of a parking lot off Dayton near Sunset. I tried to get a number but it was moving too fast in the opposite direction."

Gunny had removed his notebook and was taking notes. "I'll check out the lot tomorrow. He may work in the area." He looked across at me. "Is that all?"

"Have you ever heard of a place called the Final Frontier?"

"Holy shit, Colonel! Don't tell me you and your lady friend are spending your weekends there?"

"I take it that's an affirmative? And no, we haven't been there."

I didn't tell him where I had spent my last Saturday night.

"It's one of those anything goes sex clubs that's in a private house and we can't touch it. We got an undercover vice team from Seattle to go in a year or so back. They had some pretty wild stories to tell. But, like I said, it's private and unless we have a complaint—"

"Do you know anything about the membership? Who goes there or anything?"

"Occasionally, it'll show up in a domestic dispute, but it seems to be a fairly quiet place. You seem awfully interested. You thinkin' of joining?"

"Nothing like that. I just heard the name last week so I was wondering."

"Now you got me wondering. Did you hear the name in conjunction with the investigation you're working on?"

I didn't want to tell him some of the area's most prominent citizens were there every weekend so I tried to tap dance around the question. "I'm hearing all sorts of stuff. I'm just taking notes now, trying to sort it all out and see what I've got." Gunny nodded in agreement. At least I'd bought a little time.

"I'll give you one thing you might want to check into. We got a complaint about a year ago that the deceased was working a little too closely with one of the girls out there at the school."

"Too closely?" I leaned forward to hear him better.

"A father of one of the girls he was working with called and said he thought there was more to it than it should be."

He had my attention. "What happened?"

"Nothing. One of the suits paid a call on both of them and they denied anything was going on. Girl was over eighteen so even if it was, it wasn't illegal. I think the girl's father met Payton one night after a football game and gave him a pretty decent ass whipping. He walked around school with a busted lip and a black eye for a week. Said he got it in a fall from his boat. As I recall, we checked it out and he didn't have a boat." Gunny downed the rest of his coffee. "I've got to get back on the streets. Duty calls, you know."

We walked to the parking lot together. He was about to get into his cruiser when I handed him a folded piece of paper. "If you have a few minutes, how about running this name for me. I don't think you'll find anything, but it may help me to know he's clean."

He took the paper and, without looking at the name or making any comments, stuck it into his pocket.

I thanked him for the time and assistance. He got into his dark blue sedan and headed north on Aurora. I followed for two blocks then I cut west in the direction of town and my office.

# CHAPTER 15

I saw the car on the street across from my office when I rounded the corner. It was empty so she could have been visiting any number of businesses. There was an extremely busy women's shoe store across from me. Around the corner, one would find several jewelry stores and art galleries. I had a gut feeling that wherever she was, I'd see her prior to her leaving town.

I hadn't been in the office two minutes when the phone rang. I started to let the machine answer but I changed my mind and picked it up on the second ring.

"Mister Maxwell? Hi, it's Cathy." It was my caller from the high school. She didn't sound nearly as nervous as she had in the past. "Can I ask you a question?"

"Sure. I may not know the answer, but who knows? I may be able to successfully lie to you and you won't know the difference." There was a long silence on the other end. "I was joking about lying to you, Cathy." My joke had not been well received.

"Remember the two girls you asked me about at the library? I heard one of them talking about how she was supposed to have a part in a movie, and she wasn't going to get it because of Jeff's death."

"Did she say what movie or where it was being

filmed?" Instinctively, I knew the answer to the last part of the question.

"Yeah, she said it was in Portland."

I thanked her and said I would check it out. I also told her to call back any time she wanted. I was still sitting, doing nothing when the door opened and Anna walked in.

She was wearing a pair of black pants and a yellow jacket that looked like it came from the fall collection of a former designer of military uniforms. It was double breasted with several rows of shiny brass buttons. It had a belt with a military looking brass buckle and she had attached a small pair of pilot's wings over the top left pocket. I stood and almost felt like saluting when she entered.

"Busy?" She smiled as she spoke.

"Never so much that I can't take time out for a beautiful lady or a dive buddy. You get a double helping."

She opened a small black case she carried and pulled out several photos. "I wanted to show you the area where I went diving over in the San Juan's. You really should have taken the time to go. I'm sure you would have enjoyed it." I noticed her nails were perfectly manicured when she placed the photos in my hand. For a fleeting second, I felt the touch of her skin as she let her hand linger in mine. "I could only get half a day on Saturday and half a day on Sunday."

"Were you on a dive boat?" I thought she had booked a half-day dive for the weekend.

"No, I had to find a partner over there since you couldn't make it. All I could do was get one for a couple of hours." She gently gripped my arm. "After that, I had nothing to do for the reminder of the day."

I had to ask. "What about your husband? Does he dive?"

"Only when we go on vacation and he feels it will impress one of his clients."

"He takes his clients on vacation? That must be interesting."

"Not for me." She walked over to a large painting I had on the wall. It was a mountain man from the early days of the fur trade. He was in his winter garb. The horses behind him were loaded with pelts, and he was riding, head down, through the falling snow. She touched the lines of the horses. "This is very nice. Would you consider selling it?"

"I don't think so. I've kinda grown accustomed to it. It's one of the things I got to keep in my divorce. I'm sure you can find one very similar to it at any gallery specializing in—"

Anna quickly turned to face me. "I don't want one like it. I want this one. Will you sell it?"

She caught me off guard with the offer to buy my old painting. I knew it had no real value since it was painted by a prisoner at the Florida State Penitentiary. He was doing life for murder one, so he had plenty of time to practice his hobby. I found it when I went there to interview several inmates as part of my master's program.

"I guess it has more sentimental value than monetary, so I'm afraid I'll have to decline your offer."

"I haven't made an offer—yet."

She picked up the photos, smiled an intoxicating smile, and left.

Sometimes I wondered why I decided to go into this business. I had enough time in a number of fields in the army that I probably could have tap danced and bullshitted my way into a nice comfortable management position somewhere. I even thought about teaching school. I wanted to teach at the middle school level. I took the test for the State of Washington but I never even opened the results when they arrived at the happy little homestead where I lived at the time. If I recalled correctly, the day I got the results from the teacher's examination was the same day I opened the door to a process server who told me I was now in the middle of a divorce.

I had been retired less than a year at the time. During that year, I had been extremely hard to live with. I knew it and so did everyone else around me. I'd found out since then that it was not a unique situation. Many people who retired at a relatively young age experienced the same phenomenon. It seemed to be the number one reason for military divorces after retirement. I always wondered if my ex-wife listed that as the reason for her wanting a divorce, or if it was my being an obstinate, offensive, pain-in-the-ass.

After she filed, I took a week and visited a friend in Minnesota. He was working as a PI in a little town in the northern part of the state. His situation was very similar to mine. His marriage fell apart when he was transferred to Washington, DC, and his wife refused to leave Hawaii. I guessed if I really tried, I could blame my choice of occupations on him.

For the remainder of the afternoon after Anna left my office, I went through a book I picked up at the library. I had ordered it from the Seattle main library last week. It took me almost an hour of looking through it and cross-referencing from the index but I finally found the piece I wanted. I knew investigators who worked in offices with extensive libraries filled with books on every topic one was likely to need in this business. When I needed one, I usually went to the library down the street. If they didn't have it on the shelves, it was a simple matter to request it from another one in the system. Such was the case with the book I held in my hands.

I thumbed through the volume until I found the photo

I wanted. I took the book across the street to the office supply store and copied the page. I used them for copies, especially for books, since the library got a little spooked when they thought you were using their facilities to infringe on someone's copyright. When I got back to my office, the phone was ringing. I picked it up and found Tracy on the other end. She was crying.

"Max, do you really think Jeff was murdered?" She was trying, somewhat successfully, to get her emotions in check.

I was still standing when I answered the phone. I held the receiver and slid around to my desk where I pulled out the chair and took a seat. I had a note pad on the desk, and I made a note of the time of her call. "Settle down, Tracy. We don't know anything for certain at this point. We're going to explore all the possibilities—"

"I got a call today. He said Jeff got what he deserved." She lost it and began to cry uncontrollably.

"Do you know who it was? Did you recognize the voice?"

She answered between sobs. "No, he sounded almost like a teenager. Why would someone from the school hate Jeff so much that they would do this to me?"

If this was a kid, it went far beyond the definition of a teenaged prank. This was a vicious attack on the emotions of a woman in one of the worst times of her life. The caller knew that when he dialed the number.

"Try to remember exactly what he said. I know it'll be difficult, but I've got to know. Tell me what he said and how he said it." I heard her take several deep breaths to get herself in check.

"He said Jeff got just what he deserved. He told me drowning was too easy for someone who—" Tracy paused, sniffed, then continued. "—who fucked as many people as he did?"

I thought of the possibilities of that statement, and I wasn't convinced the caller was talking in sexual terms. "Did you hear anything in the background? Did it sound like an outdoor phone booth or have static like a cellular?"

"Maybe a cellular…in a car. I could hear sounds like he was in a car." She was regaining her composure as she tried to remember the little things that sometimes said more than the actual words. "It happened so quickly. I had just come back from meeting you. I was still taking off my jacket when the phone rang." She was suddenly quiet on the line.

"Tracy? Are you still there?"

"I think I heard a train."

"A train?"

"I'm certain I heard a train in the background. He even had to speak up at one point. I—I'm sure there was a train in the background."

I made a note of the train and the fact that she said he sounded young, perhaps a teenager. I heard my line click as another call came through. I had a system whereby if I ignored it the call was automatically transferred to my voicemail. I didn't think I needed to put Tracy on hold to take a chance on it being a call from some organization collecting old clothes for old veterans. In a moment, I saw the red light blink indicating the caller had left a message.

"You have an answering machine, don't you?" I asked.

"Yes. It still has Jeff's recording on it."

"Good. Keep the old recording on it and let the machine answer all your calls for a day or two. If this guy calls back, which I doubt he will, he'll either get spooked by the machine or he'll leave a recording of his voice.

Maybe we can find someone who'll recognize it if he does."

There was another long pause from Tracy. "Do you really think Jeff was—"

I cut her off before she could ask if I thought her husband had been murdered. "All I think right now is that you need to get your life back in order. I want you to promise you'll not answer the phone for the next three days. Go to work. Call a friend, go to dinner. Don't stay in the house by yourself. Do you have a sister or somebody you can call?"

"I have a sister in Boise. She's coming this weekend. She'll spend a week or two with me."

We talked for a few more minutes. Tracy got herself together and was no longer crying when she hung up the phone.

I glanced at my watch as I replaced the handset. It was almost four-thirty. The day had sped by. I promised Leigh I would see her prior to her going to work. If I planned to keep that promise, I had to hurry. She usually got to Hart's by five-thirty at the latest. I wanted to listen to the message that came in while I was on the phone with Tracy, and then I would leave. I hit the play button and picked up my pen in case I needed to make a note of a phone number.

"You better go ten-eight if you know what's good for you. You're getting in over your head. Just like Jeff. Ask him what happens when you get in over your head." He gave a nervous laugh. "I guess you can't very well do that, can you?" The caller snorted. "He wasn't the model citizen everyone wants him to be. Ask around. He's not the only one who's gonna die because of what he's done."

I played the recording again. I'd swear the caller was crying when he slammed the phone down. I quickly made a copy of his message on the small cassette recorder I had in my top drawer. I listened to it once more then I picked up the phone and called Leigh. I would have to take a rain check on seeing her.

Before I left the office, I made another copy of the tape and put it in the envelope with the note that I found beneath my mail slot. It didn't take a lot of imagination to see they were both from the same person.

On the way out of the office, I picked up the library book and took it with me. I wanted to drop it in the night deposit box at the library. I had always had a thing about keeping books well beyond their due date. As a kid, I almost always had to visit the librarian with a handful of change when I tried to return a book. I knew if I left it sitting my office, it would get buried under a pile of papers, and I'd wind up having to pay for it.

I pulled through the drive in area and dropped the book in the slot. I heard it make a dull thud when it hit the bottom of the metal box. As I pulled away, I wondered if I would have to pay for any damage caused by dropping it in the box.

My thoughts quickly turned from the library to a teenager named Sherman as I drove up Main Street to Ninth Avenue. I turned right and headed toward her house. It was not difficult to find since she lived with her parents in an older established neighborhood not far from the school.

The house was at the end of a street, well inside the confines of the local neighborhood. It was surrounded by houses which were built in the same time frame in the late seventies. The builders went out of their way to make them different, which seemed to make them alike in their individuality.

At one time, most had a view of the Puget Sound or the Olympic Mountains. Years of additional building had long ago destroyed their views of anything other than the house next door.

The Sherman house was painted white with green trim. Two cars were in the drive. One was a four-wheeler. The other was a small one, which I suspected belonged to Patti. I parked on the street in front of the house, left the Toyota, and walked up the drive to the front door, where I rang the bell.

It was answered by a woman in her mid-thirties. She was dressed in jeans and a sweatshirt from the University of Washington. When she opened the door, I handed her my card.

"I'm Maxwell. I called earlier about talking to your daughter."

She smiled and opened the door so I could come inside.

# Chapter 16

I was escorted into the living room. It was a modestly furnished room with a large picture window. I was certain the window once was the main selling point for the house. It was situated where, in earlier days, one could have sat on the couch and watched the ships and smaller boats on the Sound. The only thing I saw when I sat down was the house across the street.

"Thanks for letting me drop by, Mrs. Sherman. I won't take long."

She followed me into the room and took a seat across from me. "Patti'll be out here in a minute. She's doing something with her hair. Do you have daughters, Mister Maxwell?" She didn't wait for my answer. "If you don't, you can't appreciate how much time they spend trying to get their hair and clothes to look just right. Unfortunately, 'just right' for them might not meet a normal rational human being's definition of the same term."

Before I could comment, Patti came into the room. She was wearing jeans that looked like they had been the loser in a knife fight. They were skin tight, threadbare in places, and strategically ripped in others. She wore a sweatshirt from Washington State.

With her mother wearing the UW shirt, Patti's selection could have been predicated by her choice of possible colleges or a silent protest. In the state of Washington, the support of those two schools matched about like fire and gasoline.

They could have been wearing Promise Keepers and Abortion Rights shirts and not have conflicted more. Patti's hair was cut short and framed her face. It was her face that immediately caught my eye. She looked like she was several years beyond the eighteen she could legitimately claim. With the proper dress and makeup, she could walk into any club in Seattle without being carded.

I stood when she came into the room. Her mother continued to sit. "Patti, this is Mister Maxwell. He wants to talk to you."

I tried to eliminate the puzzled look on Patti's face by extending my hand. "I'll just take a few minutes of your time, Patti." I handed her my card.

She took the card and looked at it for a long silent minute. "I—I don't understand. You're a private investigator. What do you want to talk to me about?"

When I called her mother, I'd told her I wanted to speak to Patti about Jeff's death. I told her I had been retained to look into it. She didn't ask what my interests were or who had hired me. My gut instincts told me Patti would have more questions about my being there than her mother.

"I'm investigating the death of Jeff Payton."

Sometimes, it takes a word or a look to do what can't be done in a week of research or utilizing the most advanced investigative techniques. That moment in time passed across Patti's eyes when I told her why I was there.

She took a seat beside her mother before she spoke. "Why do you want to talk to me?" There was a strain in her voice.

"I'm talking to some of the students who knew him best. He was your counselor, wasn't he?"

"Yes, but he had several other girls too." She was running her hand along the back of the sofa where she sat.

"Yes I know." I pulled out my notebook and read off the names of the other girls I had gotten from Cathy. "He only worked with senior girls, right?"

"How would I know?" she answered, too quickly, and then took her time as she continued. "Uh, yes, I think that's all he did. But I'm not absolutely certain," she added.

"You and the other girls didn't plan to go to college, did you?"

Her mother answered before she could. "My husband and I have worked hard to provide a good home for Patti and her brother. We've never been able to save a lot of money. Patti's dad is in the construction business. We've had good years and bad ones. You know how it is, don't you, Mister Maxwell?"

"I'm afraid I do. I have two daughters. One is still in college; the other is trying to make it as an actress and model. She did two years of community college, then she left for Los Angeles to make her dream come true."

I was answering the mother but I was looking straight at the daughter. If I could gain a little creditability by telling a small lie, I figured what the hell.

"How did she get started? Who helped her?" Patti had taken the bait.

"You know, she graduated from high school right here in Edmonds. She'd been interested in theater long before that, but she took a lot of courses in college and then just took off to give it a shot. If she had anybody who helped her, I'm not aware of it." I took a moment to let that sink in. "She certainly didn't know anyone in this area who could do it."

"Patti's always had this notion she could become a model or an actress. We've tried to tell her how hard it is and what her chances are, but you know how these kids never believe anything a parent tells them," the mother said, talking around the young girl sitting beside her.

I made an effort to look through a notebook I carried. "I don't have my daughter's phone number or address with me, but if you'll drop by my office one day, I'll give it to you. I'm sure she wouldn't mind helping out someone from home." At eighteen, I did not need parental consent to speak to Patti. I wanted to give her time to think about the fact that I was looking into Jeff's death. If she knew anyone who might want it to happen, she certainly wouldn't tell me in her home sitting beside her mother.

We made small talk for another five minutes. It was mostly about the school and who would replace Jeff. The last thing I asked was if Patti had a boyfriend.

Again, her mother answered for her. "He's one of the nicest boys in the area. Nelson was the captain of last year's football team. It was a real tragedy for all of us for him to be with Mister—" She stopped and corrected herself. "—with Jeff when he died."

"So, you're dating Nelson Roberts?" That was the first time I put the two together. "Are you and Nelson serious, Patti?" I wanted an answer from Patti and not her mother.

"We've been dating since I was a sophomore. I—I'm not seeing any other boys—"

At that point, Patti lost it. She broke down and started to cry. I couldn't say I didn't see it coming, or didn't try to stop it. She quickly left the room.

Mrs. Sherman stood and watched as her daughter

disappeared into the rear of the house. "I'm sorry, Mister Maxwell. She's really taken Jeff's death hard. I've let her stay home from school more than I should. It's just that she starts to cry for no reason at the oddest times."

I walked to the door and turned the knob. I took one last look at the interior of the house. It was furnished in basic comfort. Large paintings adorned the walls. An entertainment center held the family television and all the assorted controllers for a variety of cable services. On a table near the couch were the obligatory family photos. One frame held two little children from an earlier year. It was probably Patti and her brother. Next to it was a more recent photo of Patti taken in front of the house. She was wearing a cheerleader's uniform and standing next to a football player whom I assumed was Nelson.

I had enough women in my life to know that females, no matter what age, didn't just start crying. There had to be a reason. I also knew, for Patti, that reason was Jeff Payton. I opened the door and left.

I stopped by my office on the way back to my apartment. There was only one call. It was from Mister Tice reconfirming my appointment to come by his shop the next morning. I picked up my unopened mail and turned out the light over my desk. I went to the bathroom where I began to wash my coffee maker when I heard the front door open. I put the pot in the sink and went back to the front.

George was standing in the middle of my office. "Evenin' Colonel."

"How ya doin', George? I haven't seen you in a couple of days. You been on vacation?"

"Yeah, I been down to Mexico. Workin' on my tan." He took his usual seat on the window ledge. "I wuz wondering if you found out anymore 'bout how the coach was killed. You still workin' on it, ain't you?"

From the first day, George had insisted on referring to Jeff's death as anything but an accident. "I'm looking into it." I took a seat since George rarely came by without staying a few minutes. I didn't want to stand while he sat.

"You talk to them girls like I said?" George leaned back on the window. This might be a longer conversation than I anticipated.

"Tell me more about the girls, George. Exactly what did you see going on between the coach and the girls at school?"

"I only seen him and them girls a couple of times. They was always closer than they should be if they was talking 'bout something from school."

"Did you ever see them doing anything more than talking? Maybe walking around after school. Something like that?"

"You know I don't really work for the school. Or nobody else, for that matter. I kinda goes where somebody wants a little help, and they pays me cash. That's how I do it at the school. Whenever they got a little job or something they don't want to call in the reg'lar cleanin' crew, they calls George. One day I was workin' over there just about sundown when I seen the coach and a girl comin' outta' his office."

"Sundown?" Depending on the time of year in this area, it could have been from three-thirty in the afternoon until about ten at night. "What time was that?"

"'Bout seven in the evening. I was going out to catch the bus home and I seen them. At first I thought it was his wife, but then I remembered she was bigger." George quickly brought his hands in front of his chest to indicate how well-endowed he found Tracy. "She was a pretty girl, though." At that point, he stopped talking and I watched as he returned to that day. "He was holdin' her hand when they walked to her car. She got in and he leaned down, stuck his head inside, and gave her a kiss. Then he did it again. They started to paw over each other right there in the car. He was runnin' his hands all up and down that little girl."

I could tell from his voice that George had a daughter somewhere in his life. I didn't say anything. I let him describe what he was seeing.

"They did that for five or ten minutes. It was like there wasn't nobody else on Earth. They didn't care who saw them. After a while, he opened the door and she followed him back to his office." George stopped talking and came back. "I 'spect we done some bad things in our life when we was in the army, Colonel. I know I did, 'specially in the Nam. But on our darkest day when we wuz dancin' with the devil and he was in the lead, we never intentionally hurt no little girls." He was almost whispering.

"How'd he hurt them, George?"

"He took away the little girl and made 'em a woman long before it was time for it to happen." He stood and placed his hand on the doorknob. "My grandmother used to say 'whatever goes over the devil's back comes back 'round under his belly.' I think maybe he was the devil, Colonel. I think maybe he really was." He turned the handle and walked out into the Edmonds night.

I watched him leave then I killed the lights and locked the door. I drove back to my apartment by way of the post office where I went through the drive-through and dropped off a couple of pieces of mail.

I parked on the street in front of my place and took my time as I got out of the truck. I had seen a small car pass me on the way from the office, but when it pulled around me, the driver was an old man. Somehow, I didn't feel threatened by him, but you never knew. I glanced back toward the street once on the walk to my front door.

I went into my kitchen and dug through the refrigerator until I found something I could unthaw and microwave. Hiding in the far corner of the bottom shelf I discovered I had a fresh bag of premixed salad and an unopened bottle of dressing. That, along with a microwaved potato and a long necked bottle of beer, was my dinner.

Leigh called me during her break at nine-thirty. We talked about ten minutes then she told me she was going shopping with one of the other ladies from work the next morning. I took that as a not-so-subtle hint to plan a night at my place alone. I agreed to meet her for an early dinner the next day.

Within an hour of hanging up the phone, I was asleep.

The next morning I grabbed a quick breakfast at the Treetopper on the way to the mall. I wanted to get there a few minutes earlier than my last visit. That would provide sufficient time to park my Toyota near the employee's car and get a couple of test shots with my video camera. I felt certain I would have an answer on film, as to why the store was losing money, by the time it opened for the day.

The employee's car was in approximately the same spot as the day before. I pulled into a parking space facing the car from an angle so I could shoot toward the trunk. That's where I expected her to put the merchandise if she was the one taking it. I took a chance on her approaching from the driver's side. If she didn't, I would have to leave my vantage point to film her.

I did my test shots, watched the replay, and adjusted for the glare of shooting through my windshield. My wait lasted less than five minutes.

She came out of the mall, carrying a shopping bag from one of the large department stores, which acted as the drawing card for the smaller shops. I took a tight shot of the name and pulled up to her face. I followed her to the car where she approached from the driver's side and opened the trunk.

Once it was open, she placed several boxes into the back of it. I was able to get a very close shot on one of the larger boxes with a name on it. That was the proof we needed. The items she was hired to sell were so specialized I doubted any other shop in the mall carried them. If she didn't have a receipt, she was in deep kim chi.

I watched her leave the car and return to the mall. I waited a few minutes, then I followed her.

When I got back in the mall, I went to the coffee shop and picked up a large cup of regular coffee. I was sitting in an extremely uncomfortable thing I was sure the mall called a chair when Bob Tice walked by on the way to his shop. If he saw me, he did not acknowledge it. After giving him time to make his presence known, I followed him to his store. Although it was still not open for business, I had arranged with him to allow me to enter. He saw me and opened the door.

My camera allowed for video playback and viewing but it was not necessary. He had a DVD recorder/player he used for training and product information in his back room. I went straight back there. He gathered the three clerks together and asked them to join us on an individual basis.

Accusing someone of stealing, even with proof, was a tricky business. If it was presented wrong, it could blow up in your face. The guilty employee could sometimes sue and collect obscene amounts of money from sympathetic juries when they felt their reputations had been ruined.

That was why I suggested we not accuse anyone.

The first employee who came back was not the one I had on tape. She was an older lady who worked part time to supplement a retirement check. This was the type of woman who would take a pen back to the bank if she picked it up by mistake.

"Good morning, my name is Maxwell. I've been retained by Mister Tice to determine if he's been losing merchandise due to theft by customers or employees."

At the mention of theft she looked in horror at her boss. "Oh, my. Have people really been taking things without paying for them? I didn't think we had a problem like that. We don't have many young people who come in, you know."

I told her I had a videotape of the guilty party putting merchandise in her car. Mister Tice reaffirmed he would not prosecute if the merchandise was returned and the guilty party agreed to never return to the store. That way, we didn't say it was an employee we suspected.

Neither she nor the young housewife who followed her into the back room asked to see the tape. It was different with number three.

Her first comment was, "I don't believe a tape like that is admissible in court."

I assured her that it was and pushed the DVD into the machine. I stalled a second, prior to hitting the PLAY button. "I think you might want to get a county police officer in here when we play this, Mister Tice."

He reached for the phone when the woman stopped him. "How do I know you'll live up to your end of the deal?" Her eyes darted between his and mine. She was a cornered mouse running scared between two cats.

I answered for him. "Because I took the tape. Neither Mister Tice nor anyone else has seen it. You return the merchandise and turn in your resignation, effective immediately, and I give that copy to you." She sat silently for a long minute. "I'll follow you out to your car if you like. I'll bring today's stuff back. We can go by you house and get the rest."

"I don't have it. I sold most of it already. I needed the money for—" I stopped her in mid-sentence. I didn't need to hear a sob story about her mother needing an operation or her kid's braces. If it was gone, it was gone.

"Give me the stuff you took today and you're out of here." I looked at Tice. I was somewhat surprised when he nodded in agreement. "If there's a back door, use that. There's no sense in the others seeing you."

After she signed her resignation, I followed her to her car where she opened the trunk and gave me the boxes she had stashed in there earlier. Once I placed them in a large box, I gave her the tape. She was crying when she drove away.

I went back inside the store and gave the box of merchandise to Mister Tice. He gave me a check for my services and I left. The other two employees were already looking around for their departed comrade.

I stopped for lunch and went back to my office where I waited for the insurance investigator to meet me.

He arrived a few minutes early. I was thumbing through the weekly newspaper, which had been delivered an hour earlier, when he opened the door.

"Maxwell? I'm Allen Getz." He handed me his card.

The only thing on it was his name and three phone numbers. With a card like that, the bearer could be anything he wanted to be, as long as he remembered how to answer his phone. "As I mentioned on the phone, you may be able to assist us in the matter of the death of Jeffery Payton."

I offered him a chair. "I'm not certain how much assistance I can provide. I already have a client who is interested in my pursuing the investigation."

"I appreciate that, Mister Maxwell. But I think you'll find the interests of your client and ours are one and the same. If there is something to Mister Payton's death other than an accident, we both need to know. You would agree to that, wouldn't you?"

Allen Getz was in his late fifties. He was probably a retired cop who got tired of the hassle of the force and the nothingness of retirement. He wore an off-the-rack suit which he picked out, put on, and wore out of the store the same day. He saved the extra thirty dollars a tailor would have charged to make it fit. If he wore his tie long enough, it was sure to come back in style. He carried an extra thirty pounds around his middle.

Getz shifted his bulk in the chair. "I checked into your background a little, Maxwell. You could make a lot more money than you do. You've got a pretty decent reputation in this business. That's pretty rare, wouldn't you say?"

"I do all right. And I generally pick who I want to work for."

"And you picked Jeff Payton? An outstanding citizen of the community and a role model for all the little kids at school. Get real, Maxwell. You've either not done your homework on this squirrel or—"

"Or what?" I demanded.

"Or nothing. I was just thinking about some of the things I've heard about him and the little lady. They led a pretty active and pretty kinky social life. Or haven't you heard?" He looked around the office. "You got any more coffee? I could use a cup." He pointed toward my cup, as if I would share as soon as he identified what I was drinking.

"There's some in the back. Help yourself. There's cups and everything you need on the sink." I had a sudden and complete dislike for the man. I would give him coffee but I'd be damned if I was going to serve it to him.

I heard him rambling around in my back room as he poured himself a cup and brought it back out to the main room. He took a drink and grinned over the top of the cup. "Not bad. I don't need all that fancy shit people drink around here. I like my coffee like I like my women. Hot, sweet, black, and strong." He flashed a stained-tooth grin over the cup as he blew across the steaming dark liquid. "How about you? Whadda you like?"

"I like people who don't try to bullshit a bull shitter. Get to the point, Getz. Why are you here?"

"Good man. Let's cut to the chase. We hold a policy on the late Coach Payton. He had one through the school and a personal one. If he died in a diving accident, we pay double. That comes to almost half a million."

"You know damn well it was a diving accident. Even if there's more to it than we know at this time."

He gave me his grin again. "Hey, Max, it's okay. You can say the 'M' word. We're both thinking murder."

Somehow, I knew I'd see that look in my dreams in the near future. "Even if it is murder, you still pay double. The last time I checked, if you're the victim of a murder, it's usually considered an accident for insurance payments."

"That's real good, Maxwell. They teach you that in detective school?"

"Is it just me, or do you piss off everyone you meet as quickly as you did me?"

"Don't feel so special, Max. It's a real talent I've developed over the years." He picked up a magazine laying on the table near the couch where he sat. "This month's edition. You must be doin' all right. Most guys I see have offices that look like barber shops. All the magazines are two years old."

"I'm gettin a shoe shine stand put in next week. It'll supplement my income."

"See, I did it again. Pissed you off and you don't even know me well enough to really dislike me yet." He laughed a long hearty laugh, placed his cup on the table, and leaned forward. I knew he was about to get serious. "Here's the deal, Sherlock. If we have enough to make a not-so-wild guess that the little woman is involved with the old man's murder, we can hold up payment for a long time. You have any idea how much money we can earn on five hundred K if we hold onto it and not pay it to the grieving widow?"

I had worked for insurance companies on previous occasions. They were all in it for the bottom line and not to give money to the family of the deceased. But I had never seen one who was so blatant in their attempt to keep from paying. "Even if she did it and gets the gallows, you still have to pay."

In Washington, a condemned person got their choice of death by lethal injection or by hanging. As soon as I said it, I got a real bad image of Tracy with a black hood over her head.

"Maybe she's not the one who actually dispatched him. We'll take conspiracy. By the time the courts sort out who shot John, we've picked up another fifty grand in investments on the policy we didn't have to pay."

As much as I hated to agree with him I knew he was telling the truth.

"And now this is where the rubber meets the road. What's in it for little Mikey Maxwell. You give me a reason to hold up payment, and my company pays you ten grand and expenses."

Good salesman that he was, he made the offer then he sat back on the couch and became as quiet as a tomb.

Once, many years ago, my former wife decided she wanted to sell real estate. She took a course and got her license. I helped her study each night and the main thing I remembered about her studies in how to sell was that every good salesman was supposed to make the offer then shut up. The philosophy was that the first person who spoke lost. I'd used it numerous times, and there was some truth to it. Her problem was that, when she shut up, she couldn't stay shut up. After four months of trying, she finally sold one house. After that, she decided to make her fortune in antiques purchased at garage sales and re-sold at exorbitant prices. When we split, she still had many of the garage-sale treasures.

Getz was sitting quietly on the couch across from me. It was a classic standoff. He probably hustled real estate in his spare time. I pulled a note pad out of my desk and began to write a letter to my daughter.

"All right, twenty grand and no expenses!" I had finished two pages and was on the third when he stood and almost yelled. "They said you were an obstinate son of a bitch. They don't know the half of it. We gonna deal or not?"

I slowly lay my pen down. "And who might 'they' be, Mister Getz?"

"The suits at the Edmonds PD. They said you think you're still in the army sometimes."

I guessed I needed to work on my image but first I needed to determine if I really gave a rat's ass. "Sit down, Getz. This won't take long." He took his seat and I slid the chair back from my desk. "First, I don't want to work for you. That part is non-negotiable. Second, you and every other slug you guys have on the payroll can bust your collected asses trying to tie the widow to his death. It's not gonna happen."

"Sounds like you're protecting her or you've already got something I need." He pulled himself off the couch and stood. "I made you a hell of an offer, Maxwell. I walk out that door and all bets are off. I'll get the same thing you have and, when I do, you don't get shit." He hesitated in order for his words to register. When they didn't have the desired effect, he tried again. "I'm serious. I might can get them to go to twenty-five if you've got something we can use."

When I didn't respond, he played his trump card. "'Course, I can always tell your friends over at the PD that you've got something they need. You don't tell them, it's obstruction of justice. They're a bunch of college boys, not guys like you and me. They're much easier to deal with, and they work a hell of a lot cheaper. They didn't beat the bricks. They spent four years' worth of their old man's money getting a degree in Criminology. A cop with a degree is about as useful as a whore with a conscience." Without looking back at me, he walked out.

The entire time he had been in my office I kept having a thought that I was missing something. I wasn't sure what it was or why I was missing it. As soon as he turned to walk out, it hit me. I had a suspect in Jeff's death. It wasn't Tracy and it wasn't even Barry, though he probably had the best motive. I picked up the phone to call Patti Sherman, and I wished I had paid more attention to George when he told me where he lived.

# CHAPTER 17

When Patti answered the phone, I immediately identified myself and asked if she was feeling better. She assured me she was, and she even laughed when I made a comment about the two different sweat shirts she and her mom wore.

"I need to ask a favor, Patti. I'm just about to wrap this thing up, and I need to talk to you for a few minutes. Do you think you can come by after school tomorrow? Around four would be best if that's all right with you." When she agreed, I asked for one more thing. "I like to keep a photo record of each of the people I interview. Do you think you can find a recent photo I can copy?" She hesitated like most young girls did as she insisted she didn't have a good one. I made a suggestion which she accepted, and we agreed to meet the next afternoon.

I couldn't believe it. It hadn't happened in more years than I remembered, but my palms were actually sweaty when I made the next call.

The call was answered on the third ring. It was a voice I didn't recognize.

"May I speak to Anna? This is Maxwell in Edmonds."

The woman who answered politely asked to put me

on hold while I waited for Anna to answer. I waited and wondered. I wondered why I was really calling her. If I needed a partner for a dive, I could call the dive shop again and get one. Just like I did when I first met Anna. I was still wondering when she answered the phone.

"Mister Maxwell, how nice of you to call. Have you decided to accept my offer?" Her voice sang through the distance.

"As I recall, you made it clear that you hadn't yet made an offer."

"Touché. Did you call to make me an offer?"

A phone conversation with this lady could get out of hand in a hurry. "As a matter of fact, I did. I—"

She didn't wait for me to finish. "I accept."

"That's pretty gutsy, you know. You don't know what I want." That was not the way I wanted the conversation to run.

She laughed. "I can only hope, but go ahead and tell me."

"I'd like to dive the Underwater Park again. I need a partner. Interested?"

"Very much so. When do you want to do it?"

"How about tomorrow at ten. I'll meet you over at the Dive Locker at nine thirty—"

"Make it nine at The Pantry and you've got a deal. You can buy me a cup of coffee and tell me why we're doing this." Without waiting for a reply, she said a cheery goodbye and hung up.

I wiped my still moist palms and called Tracy. I wanted to meet her and talk about the Final Frontier.

I called Tracy at school. Since I wasn't certain how much she could say in her office, I asked her if we could meet either at her home or my office. It wasn't difficult to convince her it was best not to have me snooping around school. We agreed to meet at six that evening. I turned down her offer to fix dinner for both of us. At this stage of the game, I still needed to be an employee and not a dinner guest.

My next job was to find George. The people who knew him all said the same thing when I called them. George just seemed to show up when something needed doing. They had all seen him in town and assumed he lived in the area but no one knew where. One man said he had seen George down by the gas storage tanks at the tank farm and speculated he might live there. I never thought of George as a street person. I always assumed he had a home of sorts, but I didn't know where to begin looking.

When in doubt, call the cops. They were supposed to know everything. I called the main switchboard and asked for Gunny. It was the beginning of his shift and he was in the office.

"Officer Reed, may I help you?"

"Gunny, its Maxwell. I wonder if you can help me. This is a real easy one, or you're not gonna be able to help at all."

"Sounds like a challenge to me, Colonel. I'm gonna lay the phone down for a minute and then you can tell me all about it. I can't put you on hold. Somebody pushed the button too hard and broke it." He lay the phone down and I could hear the normal squad room conversations. In the background, I could hear one officer telling another about a woman whom they arrested. She had been caught shoplifting with a twelve-pound turkey clutched between her thighs and under her dress. She would have made it if not for an unruly five-year-old kid who rammed his mother's shopping cart into the woman. The turkey fell to the floor in front of a store employee who, at first, thought the customer had miscarried. He called security and the shoplifter wanted to have the kid arrested for assault. Such was the activities in a small town police department.

Gunny picked up the phone. "Okay, I'm back. What is it you need?"

"There's a guy here in town named George. He comes to see me sometimes. He does a little work for people around town. I need to find him. Do you know where he lives?"

"You mean the one everyone calls Crazy George? Black guy? Wears an old army field jacket all the time?"

"That's the man, Gunny. Do you have any idea where I might find him?" I had my pen ready for directions. I expected to find him living in a basement or garage apartment behind a house on one of the main thoroughfares. I had heard him mention riding the bus several times, so I expected it to be near the regular routes.

"George's got a little place off Olympic View Drive. He's got a fantastic view of the sound. It's across the street facing the water."

I couldn't believe it so I interrupted Gunny. "I don't think we're talking about the same man. The person I'm looking for—"

Gunny laughed at me. "It's the same man, all right. I didn't believe it the first time I saw it either. He bought out there about fifteen years ago. Place is probably worth well over a million today. I can't give you the exact address but give me a minute to look at a map and I'll tell you how to get there."

I heard him open a map book and turn the pages until he got to the page with the best addresses in Edmonds on it. He gave me the two cross streets and the location of the house. I couldn't wait to get there.

It was almost four-thirty when I pulled up in front of the house that Gunny said George owned. It was an older model, probably built when a visit to Edmonds from Seattle was a day trip. There were still a few houses along the crests of the hills and the banks of the Sound that were built back in the thirties and forties. This was one of them.

The house was a small wood frame job that looked like one my grandmother should own. It was surrounded by well-manicured yards on either side and in front. Large fruit-bearing trees grew between his house and the houses on either side. Azaleas and rhodis dotted the yard, waiting for just the right moment to burst into full color. There was no garage and no car was parked in the driveway.

I walked to the front door after parking across the street from the house. I knocked, using the heavy brass door knocker. I could hear a radio or stereo playing inside. It was low enough so that the only thing I could say for certain was that the music was on.

It wasn't loud enough for me to tell what his choice of music was. From inside, I could hear someone turn down the music and walk toward the front door. When George opened the door, he was wearing his ever-present army field jacket.

George didn't seem surprised to see me standing at his front door. "Colonel, come on in." He stepped aside so I could enter.

The inside was as neatly furnished as the outside was landscaped. I stood in the one main room. Doors led off to what I assumed were two bedrooms and another opening led to the kitchen. The furnishings were old but were in excellent condition. I had the feeling George didn't get many visitors.

"I hope I'm not bothering you, George. I need you to do a little job for me if you're available."

"You know me. I'm usually available for most anything that pays a decent price." He hesitated a bit and looked hard at me. "This ain't somethin' I'm likely to go to jail over, is it?"

"No, this is something in your line of work," I assured him.

"Thas' good, cause if there's hard time involved, my price naturally goes up." He didn't smile and I didn't ask if he was joking.

I explained what I needed and we agreed on a price. He was scheduled to come by my office at four-thirty the next day. When I left George's place, I had just enough time to make it to Tracy's by six.

Tracy met me at the door. She had come from school and changed into a pair of cut-offs and a shirt that probably once belonged to Jeff. The selves were rolled up giving her a look like a star from a '60s movie.

"I hope this isn't too short notice. If it is—"

"No, not at all." She turned and walked toward her den. I followed. "I'm trying to get a little order back into my life. I've got the days covered. The nights are the hardest so I'm really glad you stopped by." She took a seat on the couch and I sat across from her in a large leather chair.

"My visit is twofold tonight. As your employee, I need to bring you up to date on what I'm doing and, as a part of that investigation, I must ask you some questions."

She had an open can of soda sitting beside her. She picked it up and took a drink. "You mean I'm paying you to ask me questions?"

"For the next few minutes I would say that's a pretty good description." I opened the folder I brought with me and extracted several sheets of paper. These were the daily reports I always kept for clients. They covered who I talked with, what I talked about, and any expenses were listed.

Tracy took them, glanced quickly at the forms, and placed them beside her on the couch.

"Okay, that was the easy part. Now for the real reason you came. Let's talk about the Final Frontier. How in depth do you want to go?" She took another drink and waited for my answer.

"I'm not sure. Let's just start and see where it goes."

For the next hour she talked and I listened as she described the lifestyle she referred to as "alternative." She gave me the reasons and rationale she and Jeff used to go for the first time, why they became members, and how they happened to become even closer friends with Marge and Barry. She explained their use of computers for cybersex. Her explanation was the same as the one I got from Marge.

At one point, she excused herself to go into her bedroom. After a few minutes, she brought out a large photo album filled with vacation photos of the four of them. The photos were in a variety of combinations of couples, singles, and threesomes. To look at them, one would think this was two couples on a vacation in Mexico. Because there were so many combinations, the viewer might have a difficult time determining who was with whom. None were as explicate as the ones I found and took when I was going through Jeff's belongings.

"Did you know Jeff and Marge were seeing each other away from the club?"

"Not at first, but then after a while, I guess I figured it was happening."

"What did you do?"

"Nothing."

"Why not? Wasn't that breaking one of the rules?"

"It was. But, by that time, Jeff and I had even stopped having sex with each other so it didn't really matter."

"Were you seeing Barry on the side?" I was trying to make notes but it was almost like trying to keep score at a basketball game.

Tracy laughed. "No. Believe it or not, I was faithful. I didn't do anything or anybody behind his back. I thought that was the whole reason we were involved in the Frontier. To keep that sort of thing from happening."

"Tracy, do you know if Jeff was having an affair or anything with anyone other than Marge?"

"You went to the Frontier last week, Max. Do you think the people there would describe themselves as having affairs? It's sex, with a capital SEX. That's it. Nothing more, nothing less. If it's with a partner you bring with you or someone you meet for the first or fiftieth time, it's still the same. S-E-X."

She closed the book and took it back to the bedroom. When she returned, she had a slick, four-color brochure that she handed me. "You think this is limited to Edmonds? Look at this. There's a National Swinger's Convention every year in Las Vegas. There'll be five or six hundred couples there. It's big business and it's worldwide. We talked about going again this summer. I think we would have too, if—" She stopped talking without filling in the blank. She regained her composure. "We never asked anyone to accept or condone the lifestyle. It's not something we talked about to those who weren't involved. It may sound crazy, but to us it was no more than belonging to a Saturday night bowling league or a group who was involved with boating or diving. It was just something we did."

I had tried to get her to talk about Jeff's activities outside the area, specifically Portland, but with the exception of her mention of it last week, she did not broach the subject.

Tracy stopped and looked at me. "I've been doing all

the talking for the last hour. Why don't you tell me what you've found out?"

I pulled a copy of the report from my case and placed it on the table by my chair. "I've got some pretty interesting leads I'm following—"

Tracy cut in. "Does that mean you think Jeff's death was not accidental? How could it be anything else? There was no one else down there, except Jeff and Nelson—" She stopped and picked up the reports. "Was there anyone else diving down there that day?"

"That's one of the things I'm looking into." I tried to shift from that point. "Do you know how much insurance Jeff had?"

"I got a letter from the insurance company last week. They said they were processing the claim. He had a policy at the school and one we paid individually. I'm not entirely sure of the total. Should I be?"

"I think that's something you need to bring to the attention of your lawyer. You do have a lawyer, don't you?"

"Yes, he's got Jeff's will. I guess I need to take the insurance papers to him too, huh?"

I sat back in the chair. I felt better talking about the Final Frontier than the next item on my agenda. "Tell me about the girls Jeff was counseling. Did you know any of them?"

"They were students. I knew all of 'em." She reached for her drink. "How well should I know them?"

I hesitated. "I guess a better question would be to ask what type of counseling Jeff did for them. Was it for college or jobs or what?"

For the first time, Tracy did not have a readily available answer. She took her time as she weighed her response. "He did what every other person who really cared about the students did. He helped them in any way he could. Sometimes, it went beyond choices for college or whether to go to work for Nordstrom's or some pet shop when they graduated."

I leaned forward. "What type of choices fell into the 'other' category?"

"We live in a very exciting time. There are things happening now that were not even on the drawing boards when you and I were in high school. Kids today are faced with choices we never even dreamed of. And the consequences for a wrong decision may be life altering." Tracy's eyes flashed with a passion when she talked about the students at the school.

"Give me an example."

"Let's take the obvious. Sex. It's more prevalent than anyone not in school or involved with the kids can imagine. And with it goes the dangers and responsibilities. Every year we have at least five girls who are pregnant when they graduate. A couple will get married, the others may keep the child or give it up for adoption. In the last five years, we've had three kids die from AIDS. I know of two in the senior class this year who are HIV positive. They'll probably be gone in five years." She stood, walked to the bar, and opened it. Without asking, she poured two drinks. "How many of your high school graduating class has died from AIDS?" she asked as she handed me the drink.

We sat quietly for a minute. I was the first to speak. I pulled the folder with the info on the girls I knew Jeff had been counseling and placed it on the edge of the chair. "I'd like you to take a minute and tell me anything you know about these girls."

We went through them, one at a time. Each had a story about the same as the one before her. They were trying to get into college and wanted to get a scholarship or grants to cover it. Most didn't qualify for academic scholarships and few would get grants, so it seemed like loans and Daddy's money if they wanted to move beyond the cosmetic counter at the mall. I saved Patti Sherman for last.

"And this one. What can you tell me about her?" I handed Tracy the name on a piece of paper.

"Little Miss Sherman." There was a slight note of sarcasm in her voice when she spoke. "Every class has one. She's the one who could make it on her looks alone if the world was fair. She has the face, the personality, and the body. She even has talent. This is the girl from the class who wants to go to New York and be a model or Hollywood and be an actress. The problem is that there are ten thousand more like her in line already."

"What's stopping her from taking a chance?"

"A concerned mother. A small-town mentality. A lack of money. A boyfriend who's insanely jealous and overbearing. Shall I go on?"

"No. I get the picture. What was Jeff's advice to her? Do you know what he was trying to do for Patti?"

"He never talked much about specifics. They all seemed to run together after a while. He was trying to get her a drama scholarship, if I recall. I can check on all of them if you think it's necessary." She finished her drink and got up to get another. "What do you think they have to do with his death?"

I watched her refill our two glasses. "I have to look at everyone in his life if I'm to find out what happened. These just happen to be students he spent more time with than any of the others." When she didn't respond and returned with the drinks, I knew she bought that excuse.

We talked for a few more minutes about things having nothing to do with Jeff or the school. I asked one last question before I left. "Give me your definition of 'insanely jealous.'"

"You mean Patti's boyfriend?"
I nodded and she told me.

# CHAPTER 18

When I arrived at The Pantry, most of the tables were already filled with locals having breakfast. Many of the townspeople came in just prior to opening their businesses and occupied a table while they drank coffee and read the day's mail. A few were decent tippers so the waitresses didn't mind keeping their cups filled. There were two people in line ahead of me so I put two quarters in the pull-tab machine and came up a loser as usual.

I was standing at the machine with my back to the door when I felt Anna enter. She was wearing Calvin Kline jeans and a sweatshirt from a vineyard in the Napa Valley. When she stepped into the room, it became hers.

"Am I fashionably late yet?" she asked as she came to stand beside me.

"Right on time."

"Damn! I could leave and come back if you like. My mother said a lady should always be fashionably late wherever she went."

"Somehow, I can't see her talking about a hash house in Washington."

"You're probably right. I'll save it for next time."

Before I could ask what she meant by "next time,"

the young woman serving as hostess and waitress-in-training took us to our booth. As Anna slid across the seat, I ordered a cup of coffee for me. "I'm afraid you'll have to order your own latte. I haven't broken the code on how to do it yet."

She gave the waitress her order and settled back in the booth. "What are you looking for today? Are you still trying to find out what happened to your friend?" Before I could answer, she added, "Or how it happened?"

"I think it's more of the latter. I know he drowned. It's the how and the why that still bothers me."

She took a sip of her too-hot latte. "That's interesting. I would have thought you'd be adding a 'who' to that list of unanswered questions by now."

"Who?"

She sat her cup down. "We're going to play enough games, Max. This shouldn't be one of them. I don't think you believe Jeff simply went out there, made a mistake, and paid for it with his life. You think there's more to it than that, and I believe you'll find the person if there is one to be found." Her face went from serious to light in a matter of seconds. "I'd like to think you invited me to dive with you because you enjoy my company." She took a drink from her coffee. "You do enjoy my company, don't you?" She finished her drink, smiled, and placed her empty cup on the table.

I knew I was on the spot, so I did the only thing I could think of at the time. I put a five-dollar bill on the table and we left.

I had parked outside in front of The Pantry on the street. Anna was across the street in the public parking lot. I walked her to her car and watched as she pulled out and headed to the waterfront. I crossed the street to my Toyota. As I pulled into the traffic, I saw George cross the street. He was already on the job I had given him.

Anna and I changed into our dry suits at the Dive Locker. Both our tanks were full, so I put the gear in the back of my Toyota and drove us back to the park. I was still using the same suit I purchased several years earlier. Anna was in a different one than the one she used during the previous dive. It was equally fashionable with a palate of bright colors. She was still wearing the diamond studs in her ears.

At the park I unloaded and we quickly put on our tanks and stood at the edge of the water. I pulled the plastic covered map from my bag and held it between us.

Anna held one edge of the map with her right hand. She propped her left arm casually on my shoulder as she stood close to me. "Have you got a plan? Or will we be down there dancing in the dark again?"

The Edmonds Underwater Park had become such a tourist and diver attraction that the entire park was mapped with streets and monuments having names. It was virtually impossible to get lost or hurt if the diver used his or her head and a little common sense.

Unfortunately, each month the local rescue vehicles made several trips to the hospital or the morgue with those who didn't.

"I want to get to the old dry dock when there's no ferry either coming in or going out. It'll be about forty-five feet deep today with the high tide. If we follow the buoys, we can go in along Enchantment Way to Telegraph and turn south to the concrete pilings. That's our first stop. Then west to the old dry dock."

"Is this how you planned military operations when you were in the army?"

I laughed. "I guess I do have a lot of that left in me, don't I?"

"Is that where he died? The dry dock?"

"According to the reports, that's where it happened. I

want to see it one more time before I talk to his dive buddy from that day."

"Will that be our last stop for the day?" Anna turned to face me. "I mean underwater."

I was caught a little off guard and then I realized I had not given her any indication of how long we would be in the water when I called her. "I'm sorry. I should have asked if you had anything else scheduled for today when I called. Are you in a hurry to get somewhere when we're finished here?"

Her hand slid slowly down my arm. "I wouldn't call it a hurry so much as just being anxious." She smiled, inserted her regulator, and adjusted her mask.

I did the same and we entered the water.

It was an easy swim out to the first buoy marking the route along Enchanted Way. The water temperature was usually in the forty-eight-to-fifty-degree range, so it was not uncomfortable once we actually got underwater. Anna led the way and waited for me at the marker for our first checkpoint. The ferry had almost completed loading, so we had about ten minutes before it would clear the dock. I wanted to use that time checking the debris around the concrete pilings on Telegraph and then go to the old dry dock when the ferry was gone and we didn't have to worry about the churning propellers stirring up the water, or us, if we ventured too close.

As we neared the crusty cement, we passed an area known as the Jungle Gym. It reminded me of an area where I had once trained with the army Special Forces. We were taught how to place underwater demolition charges on structures that looked a lot like many of the areas in the park. That might have been one of the reasons I didn't dive it more often than I did. It wasn't from flashbacks or anything as exotic as that but rather, each time I got near those sunken pieces, I always spent a few minutes mentally placing charges and blowing them up.

At the Enchantment buoy, Anna motioned for me to take the lead. I acknowledged her, swam around her, and motioned for her to follow. I stopped at the first cement piling and waited for her to swim to my side. When she floated almost motionless beside me, I began to run my hand along the exposed steel rods in the cement. Each was covered with barnacles and algae. After sliding my hands along most of the exposed rods, I checked my watch. The ferry dock should be clear so I motioned in that direction to Anna.

We swam to the old dock and stopped. We had a limited visibility of about ten feet around the dock. Since I wanted to see the dock up close I had an underwater light with me. As soon as we stopped, I pulled it from my harness and switched it on. We immediately attracted several medium sized curious fish that stopped by to see us. Anna reached out and gently touched one on the nose before it satisfied its curiosity and swam back to the safety of the darkness.

Before I could shine the light toward the dock, Anna tapped me and held up her slate where she had written a message. It said, *Looking for?*

She handed the slate and marker to me. I took it and wrote, *Not sure!*

She nodded and gave me a thumb up, indicating she understood. She followed as I began to shine my light on the exposed wood, steel beams, and other pieces that made up an abandoned and sunken dry dock.

According to the report, we were in the spot where Jeff had been trapped. I moved the light across each piece. All were heavily encrusted with the barnacles of fifty years of seawater. I was following one long piece of exposed steel rod approximately two inches in diameter. It was bent in several places and, like everything else, it was covered with barnacles. I was about to stop when my light flashed across something that should not have been in that place at that time. I ran my hand across the rod and gave a little kick with my flippers to take me beneath it for another look. As I emerged on the other side, Anna held up her slate.

She had written, *Find it???*

I hesitated and then nodded yes. It had taken another trip to the park but I finally knew how Jeff died. What was more, I felt certain there was a "who" and I knew the person's name. Now all I needed was the "why."

I was still lost in my own thought when Anna swam beside me. I was about to motion for us to return when she gave a slight kick and pulled up in front of me. With her facing me less than a foot away, she held up her finger to indicate I was to watch her. She then pointed to her mask and regulator and did the same to mine. My first thought was that something was wrong with her line, and I started to give her mine when she stopped me.

Once again she went through the signs. Anna pointed to indicate I should watch her. She then pointed to her mask and hose, and then to mine.

Slowly she removed her mask. Her eyes remained open in the water. Anna reached across and slowly lifted my mask. She waited until she made certain I wouldn't do anything rash then she removed her regulator. While holding her breath she reached over and removed my regulator.

Anna placed her hand behind my head and drew me to her where she pressed her lips to mine. With our mouths forming a virtual air lock she slid her tongue across my lips.

I'd been in a lot of strange situations in my life, but at that moment I couldn't remember any that involved so many senses and emotions. Before I had a chance to either respond or drown, Anna broke the kiss, put her regulator in her mouth, and pulled her facemask back in place. I did the same and found myself treading water at the forty feet, level with Anna.

She took her slate and began to write. Her note was in keeping with the last few minutes. It said, *Through—for now!* When she was certain I had read it, she swam by me and headed toward the ropes leading to Enchantment Way. I couldn't help but think what an appropriate name they had given the route we took.

Once we made it to the small rocky area the locals called a beach, Anna was quick to remove her tanks and other gear. I followed suit and carried the equipment to my Toyota. When all was secured, the only thing left to do was for us to get into the confines of the vehicle and drive back to the Dive Locker and Anna's car. Although I was thinking about what I had seen at the Underwater Park, my thoughts were equally taken by Anna. I knew one of us had to say something.

I glanced over at her as I drove. Anna was staring straight ahead. Her eyes were on the road in front of us. "I've been in some interesting situations on dives before, but—"

Before I could finish, she spoke quietly without looking at me. "What a lovely choice of words. You see that as an 'interesting situation.' I thought you might find it a bit more than that. I certainly did."

"No, that's not what I meant. It's just that—"

"I find you extremely fascinating, Mister Maxwell. I'm not certain why, but I do. I'm sure we have very few things in common but that doesn't matter to me. At least not now. You have a lot of work ahead of you in the next few days or weeks or whatever it takes to resolve the death of your friend." She turned in the seat to face me. "You may very well need someone to talk to during that time. Perhaps another dive. I'm home most of the day, so you can call anytime you want to or need to. I sleep alone so you can even call me at night if that's an option for you." Even driving as slow as possible, the parking lot for the Dive Locker was suddenly in front of us. I pulled beside her Lexus and stopped.

We were alone at the rear of the lot. There were no other cars around us. I wasn't certain if that was a good thing or not. At least we both were still wearing our seat belts when I stopped. Before I could turn off the ignition, I heard the sharp click as Anna unbuckled. It took a single movement to release my belt, turn in the seat, and take Anna's face in my hands. I pulled her to me and finished the kiss we started in the depths of Brackett's Landing.

# CHAPTER 19

I watched Anna pull from the parking lot after we both had gone inside the Dive Locker to change. Her car had barely disappeared across the railroad tracks when I saw a second car that immediately grabbed my attention. It was a small Firebird. Its single male occupant didn't look my way as he pulled out and sped away in the direction leading out of town. As soon as he left the lot, I saw another familiar figure standing near the entrance. It was George.

The more I learned about him, the more I wondered why people referred to him as Crazy George.

I drove straight to my office. If my hunch was right, George wouldn't be far behind me. It would take him about fifteen minutes to walk so I went across the street and ordered two sandwiches and a couple of bottle of imported beer and brought them back to the office. As soon as I returned and placed the drinks in my small refrigerator, my door opened and I heard the familiar voice of George as he called to me.

"You in here, Colonel? It's George."

"I'm back here, George. I'll be out in a minute." I pulled the drinks back out and carried them and the sandwiches out to the main area.

"I hope you didn't eat lunch yet. I got us a couple of sandwiches and some beer."

Without waiting for a response, I handed him one of each. He didn't even glance at the type of sandwich or brand of beer before making it his lunch. He didn't speak again until both were gone. "I watched that boy come and go today. He works at the cabinet shop down by the boat yard. His car was like you told me. I got the tag number." George reached into the pocket of his ever-present army field jacket and pulled out a small piece of paper. Neatly printed on it was a tag number. It was the same as the one I had copied earlier from the parking lot at the Dive Locker. He handed me another, longer, sheet of paper.

"What's this?" I asked as I looked at what appeared to be an inventory of some type.

"It's a list of everything in his car. Kind of a bonus. I thought you might could use it."

I looked at the list. It was detailed enough to include the brand of chewing gum wrappers on the floor. "I won't even ask how you managed to get inside his car," I said as I continued to read. Halfway down the list was two items that immediately caught my attention. One was listed as the end flap from a box of .38-caliber bullets, and the other was a brochure from what George had listed as a club called the Final Frontier. Other items on the list were receipts for tuition from the community college he attended, an appointment slip from the local Planned Parenthood clinic, and a pair of rusty handcuffs.

I finished my beer and paid George for his day's work. He tucked the money in his pocket and walked toward the door. As he opened it, he turned back to face me. "I knew that coach didn't die on his own. And now you don't think he did neither, do you?" Without waiting for my response, George left the office.

With less than two hours until Patti Sherman was due

in my office, I had to hurry if I wanted things to work. Before I could make my first call, the phone rang. It was Leigh.

"Are we alone?" Her voice had a sexy, still sleepy sound to it. "If we are, tell me what you'd like for me to do to you."

I thought of where I'd been and what I'd done in the last two hours and I wondered if her female radar had picked it up. "We are alone, but if I told you, the phone company would have to come out and replace the melted receiver."

"Go ahead; give it your best shot. I've got a spare phone I can loan you."

This was not the time to play with Leigh's head or her heart. I quickly got into a serious mode. "I'd love to, but duty calls. I'm up to my ass in alligators. I'll have to call you back."

I heard her stretch and moan softly in the bed. "I slept late today. It just felt so good I couldn't leave the bed. I feel somewhat decadent." She was talking around a yawn. "Will I see you tonight?"

"Probably, but I'll have to call. If you're already at work, I'll leave word there."

We talked for a few minutes then I heard her line click as another call was coming in. "Take your call. I'll talk to you later."

As soon as we broke the connection, I dialed the number for Nelson Roberts. It was time for the two of us to meet face-to-face.

His mother answered the phone. She seemed like a nice lady but she was very protective of her son. I identified myself as a friend of Coach Payton's and said I needed to talk to Nelson. She told me he wasn't home.

"I really would like Nelson to call me. I'm trying to finish some paperwork and I need to speak to him for a few minutes." I waited to see if she would be more cooperative this time than last. She wasn't.

"You know he goes to school and works. He doesn't have time to..."

I didn't want to do it but it was time to play a trump card.

"Let me leave a message for him. Tell Nelson I'm talking to Patti this afternoon and to Planned Parenthood tomorrow." My hope was his mother didn't realize I could talk to Planned Parenthood about anything I wanted to as long as it didn't pertain to someone else. Getting information about her son and any dealings he may have had with them was like getting a friendly voice at the IRS. It couldn't be done. "Please give him the message. He'll know what I'm talking about." I certainly hoped he would and further hoped he would share the information with me.

As I placed the phone back on the holder, I remembered something Anna had said earlier in the day. When we were looking at the map of the Underwater Park and I was giving her the route we were to take, she asked if I planned all my military operations like that. As I looked at the yellow pad in front of me, I had been doodling notes about Jeff's death and about those involved. The name of each person I had spoken to was drawn across the bottom of the page. I had placed a little box around each with the top of the box forming an arrow pointing toward the top of the page. If this was a battle plan those names would be the units in movement and at the top of the page was the objective. All my names and arrows pointed to the top and to the one name I had written up there. Without thinking of it, I had made a battle plan. All that was left now was to assault the objective and capture it.

I was still looking at the paper when the door to my

office opened and Patti Sherman entered. When I was in high school, she would have been voted best looking, cutest, Miss Personality and the Prom Queen. She would have gone on to finish college and then married a guy who worked in a bank. After twenty years, he'd be a branch manager and she'd be president of her kid's PTA. I wondered as she cautiously entered my office if her life would ever be that simple.

"Mister Maxwell, you wanted to see me?" She spoke barely above a whisper. She was holding the framed photo as I had requested. It was of her and her boyfriend, Nelson Roberts. They were standing beside his car.

"Yes, thanks for coming." I stood and met her in the middle of the room. "Why don't you have a seat? This'll just take a few minutes." I steered her toward the couch and watched as she took a seat. I sat in the chair across from her. I had already placed a folder containing everything I needed on the table by my chair. "Patti, you know I've been hired to look into Coach Payton's' death. That's why I've been asking so many questions of you and your friends."

"Did you find out there was something wrong with him when he died, or what?"

"Oh, I found out a lot of things. I'm trying to get a second opinion on some of them and a confirmation on others. All I'm trying to do is find out how a man who was a diving instructor died in shallow water that close to shore. That's something I'd like to know." I took her arm, held it a little tighter than I normally would, and forced her to make eye contact. "That's something we'd all like to know, don't you think?"

She moved ever so slightly when she answered. It was a move more associated with nervousness than discomfort. "I—I thought he drowned. That's what—what everyone said."

"Is that what Nelson told you? He was there. If anyone knows, it should be him." I didn't wait for her to answer. I took the folder and opened it. "Patti, I need to ask you some hard questions. I thought they might be some you didn't want to answer in front of your mother. That's why I asked you to meet here. You're over eighteen so you don't need her permission to speak to me, but if you'd like, we can talk at your home or I can invite her down here." I failed to mention that she didn't have to answer anything I asked her. I hoped she didn't realize that from watching too many cop shows on television.

Patti thought for a minute and then told me to go ahead. We talked for a few minutes about school and what she planned to do after graduation. "Was Jeff trying to steer you toward a particular college?"

"No. He said I might want to consider a community college for a year and then go to a four-year one in California. He said USC or UCLA. I always wanted to be a model or an actress, you know," she added, almost as an afterthought.

"Was he trying to help you get into the business? Trying to introduce you to agents or anything like that?"

For the first time, Patti sat without speaking.

"Did he mention any of his friends who were in the film business? Maybe down in Portland?" I pressed.

At the mention of Portland, Patti showed her nervousness. If we had been playing a board game, I would have moved her game piece into the "captured and compromised" holding area. "We met went to meet them—" She stopped, as if she realized she was revealing more than she wanted me to know.

"You and Jeff drove down to Portland to meet them," I finished for her. "Except you never got to Portland. You stayed in Vancouver. At the…" I took out a copy of a motel charge slip from a large complex on the

Columbia River separating Washington and Oregon. "...you stayed at The Cliffs." I held the slip. Even with Patti over eighteen, Jeff had been careful not to cross the state line with her.

Patti began to cry. "Oh, God. Please don't tell my mom. She'd die."

I waited for her to regain a little composure. As I did so, the phone rang. I had set the system to answer on the first ring, so it didn't bother us. I stood and went to the back room, where I got her a soda and me a cup of coffee. When I got back into the room she had stopped crying. "Do you want to tell me what Jeff did or do you want me to tell you?"

When Patti didn't answer, I took a photo out of the folder. "I had to go through Jeff's personal effects after he died. I found some photos." I held them in my hand. "I think you know which ones I talking about."

I watched as a transformation began in front of me. Patti went from a vulnerable high school girl to a young woman about to defend her honor. And that of her dead lover.

"I'm very proud of those photos. I think Jeff did a good job when he took them. He was using them to get me modeling jobs. That's why we were going to Portland. We met some producers from Hollywood, but they came to Vancouver."

I saw it coming but I had to ask the obvious. "Were they there when Jeff took the photos?"

Patti hesitated a little too long. It gave her time to think for perhaps the first time. "Well, yes. But they said it was routine for the producer and director to be in the room if any nude shots were being taken."

"Did they ask for anything else? Did you make any videos either alone or with Jeff?"

Patti jumped to her feet. "What do you think I am,

Mister Maxwell? Jeff was looking out for my best interests. He wouldn't let anyone else do anything with me. They just did what directors would do on any movie."

I motioned for her to sit. "I'm sure you're right, Patti, so let's talk about you and Jeff." I waited for a moment for her to calm herself. "How long had you and Jeff been having sex?"

"You make it sound so clinical. Animals have sex. Jeff and I made love." She took a drink from the soda. The transformation was complete. High school Patti had been replaced by Cosmo Patti. "The first time was just after my birthday. In February. It was raining one afternoon after school. I stayed for a session with him and he offered to take me home. It was a Friday and I was going to spend the night with my friend Cathy 'cause my parents were going out of town." She took another sip from the soda as she mentally returned to that afternoon. "He was wonderful. Not like—" She stopped short.

"Not like Nelson Roberts?"

"No. Not like anyone. Nelson, or anyone else."

I didn't know if her smile was for shock effect or to see if I would ask for a number.

"Did Jeff ever mention the Final Frontier to you?"

"You mean the wife swappers' club? No, he didn't mention it. Everybody at school has heard rumors about it. But we all know it's not real. Why?"

"No, it's real all right, and it's located about an hour's drive east of here. Did you know Jeff sometimes went there?" I knew I had crossed a thin line possibly protecting a part of Tracy's life she might not want to be public, but if my plan of attack was correct, very little about Jeff and Tracy would be secret after today.

It was an emotional Patti who stood and almost yelled at me. "No! He didn't go there. He wouldn't. He said he had everything he wanted with me."

She began to cry much harder, now that the truth was coming out. As I watched her, I thought of the many other photos I had seen of Jeff. Some of them with Marge and some with classmates of Patti's.

Patti was on such an emotional overload, I decided to try another tactic. "How often do you have to go to Planned Parenthood?"

"I started going after—" She swallowed hard. "You know, after Nelson got sick."

I sat back, took a deep breath, and let Patti do the same. "Patti, I know this has been very painful for you but it's all been necessary if I'm to find out what really happened to Jeff. I hope you know that everything you told me is just between the two of us." I hated to tell her the caveat to that. "But if I find out that Jeff's death wasn't an accident, you may be asked some of these same questions by the police. You do realize that, don't you?"

She gave a slight nod.

Patti had told me enough to prove my theory about Jeff's death. It was now time for the final assault.

It was a little after five when Patti left my office. As soon as she left, I dialed the number to my old pager and punched in a message to call me. I depressed the button on the phone to break the connection and immediately dialed Gunny. When he answered, I told him what I was doing and how I wanted him to assist. He agreed and I prepared for the next phase of the operation.

I was standing behind my desk when the phone rang. I caught it after the first ring. It was George. "You called me, Colonel?"

I had given George my pager and told him I would call as soon as I wanted him to help with the remainder of the operation.

"I need to make one more call then I think I'll need you here at the office. Are you still in town?"

"I'm down at the fishing pier, not far from where they found the coach." George had a way of pronouncing Jeff's old title as if it had an "r" in it. He made it come out "coarch."

"Stay close and I'll call you back within an hour." I started to ask if he had money to eat, but decided against it. A man who could afford an Olympic View address could afford a meal in Edmonds.

The light on my machine was still blinking, indicating I had a message I had not yet retrieved. With any luck, it would be the one I wanted. Before I listened to it, I pulled my recorder from the drawer. I wanted to keep a record of the voice if it was the right one.

As soon as I activated the recorder and pushed the blinking red button, I knew I had the right one. The caller left a number where he could be reached. After making certain I had a copy of the call on tape, I hit the delete button and called the number he had left.

He answered on the third ring.

"Maxwell here. I think it's time we had a little talk."

# Chapter 20

I had a table overlooking the water in the far corner of Hart's. I asked Leigh to keep the area as uncluttered as possible while I was there. Although the restaurant was beginning to fill with the early dinner crowd, she did her best and a single diner was placed at a table near us. He was at the table directly in front of mine but he had his back to ours. I was nursing a tonic and lime when Leigh approached the table with my dinner companion.

"You Maxwell?" Nelson Roberts tried to sound older and tougher than his one year pass anything ending in a teen. He pulled out his own chair and slid his lanky frame into place.

I nodded. "I'm surprised this is the first time we've met. I usually try to get to know the people who take shots at me."

Before he could respond, the young man who was pouring water stopped by our table and filled both our glasses.

"I didn't invite you here to talk about what a lousy shot you are," I continued when the waiter left, "but we'll get around to that in a minute. What I want to talk about is your late friend Jeff Payton. He *was* your friend, wasn't he?"

Nelson looked casually out the window at the ferry making its way across the sound. "Sure he was. Both of them. He was my coach when I was in high school. We were diving buddies, too."

"How would you describe Jeff? Did all the guys at school like him?"

"I guess so."

"How about the girls? Did they like him?" I paused for effect then added, "Did they like him as much as he liked them? He was pretty close with a couple of them, wasn't he?" I pulled out the photos and made two stacks of them. I held one group so Nelson could see they were of nude girls but he couldn't tell who they were. "Let's see…" I said as I thumbed through them. "I guess Donna was his favorite. Or maybe it was Gail? He had two really nice pictures of her." I took my time and looked at them, and then I put the first stack of photos in my coat pocket. I still held the other stack. "How about Patti Sherman? How well did he like her?" I turned the stack toward Nelson so he could see they were of Patti.

"You son of a bitch," he growled through clenched teeth. "Where did you get those pictures?" He made a fist and bounced it firmly but quietly on the edge of the table. "This is none of your business."

"Oh, but it is. It's complements of you and your bad aim. You missed with your pistol and your car. That was two chances to take me out. I guess it's a good thing we don't dive together, isn't it?"

"Whadda you mean?"

"Simple. I wouldn't want you to kill me like you did Jeff. How's that?" I leaned forward so he could hear me. Leigh was seating another couple at a table near us but I was certain they couldn't hear.

"Kill Jeff? Are you fucking crazy? Jeff drowned. Everyone knows that. It was an accident."

Nelson took another sip from his water. Was he thirsty or was it an act to stall for time to collect his thoughts. I'd soon find out. When he sat the glass down, I heard him crunch a piece of ice with his molars. As I watched him, a smile slowly broke out on his somewhat-handsome face.

I had seen a smile like his only once before. It was on a man who had killed his wife and her mother by setting fire to his house at Fort Hood, Texas.

"You were on a roll there for a minute," I said. "You got two out of three. He did drown and everyone knows about it. You blew it on the accident part."

"You weren't there. You don't know." His cockiness was getting offensive.

"You're right. I wasn't there at the time but I went back to the site. Twice. Something wasn't right the first time, and I couldn't figure it out. Then I looked at the autopsy photos again. Jeff had a broken wrist. The bone was ground down and had some minor cracks in it."

Behind Nelson, the man ordered another drink, and it was brought to him. Our water glasses were refilled.

"Some junk fell on him. That must've crushed his wrist." Nelson's eyes flashed as he looked at me. I could see a house fire in them.

"What do you mean, 'must have'? You were there. You were the one who pulled him out. Don't you know what happened?"

"Damn right, I do. And I told the cops everything that happened. Why don't you go find the other diver that was down there? He—"

I didn't let him finish. "Other diver? What other diver? You and Jeff were the only two down there." I didn't want to continue but I had to. "Weren't you?"

Outside the restaurant, the running lights on the ferry, crossing the Puget Sound from Edmonds to Kingston, flashed across the black water as it pulled away from the Edmonds dock.

Onboard were commuters who pulled their cars into parking spaces then ran up the stairways to the coffee shop. There they spent money for yet another latte or cappuccino or a coffee concoction that took longer to order and make than it did to drink. The deep, throaty fog horn blasted a warning to all boats in the area and brought me back to the reason I was sitting across from the person I had been certain had killed Jeff. But as I sat with him, I began to get a nagging feeling that some pieces of the puzzle had been trimmed to fit.

Nelson squirmed. "There was another guy down there. I saw him for just a minute."

He looked around. Was he getting spooked?

"Who was he?"

"How the hell am I supposed to know? Look, let's go through this one more time and then you get out of my life forever." He glanced around for a waiter. "I need something to drink besides water." He turned back to me. "Buy me a beer."

"Sorry, sport. Not tonight and especially not here. When you can give them a real ID with your photo on it that says you're at least twenty-one, I'll buy the first round. Till then, if I buy, it's soda or coffee. Take your choice."

Without waiting for the waiter, he continued with his account of the incident at the underwater park. "We'd been down about thirty minutes when I first saw the other guy. The water was really bad that day so I couldn't see too far. I thought it was just some other divers. I've seen other people down there on occasion." He scanned the restaurant, as if he wanted to make sure no one else heard the story. "This guy swims by us once or twice like he's checking us out. I wrote a big question mark on my slate and showed it to Jeff. He just kinda shrugged, like he didn't know who it was either."

Leigh walked by us and slid her hand across the back of my neck. The movement was so slight I doubt the couple she was seating at a table overlooking the water noticed. The quick touch was enough to make me wish my time with Nelson was over and Leigh and I were headed home.

"About that time I had a problem with my regulator," Nelson said. "I must have bumped something in the park, because it was almost knocked off the tank. I pulled the tank off and let it sit on the bottom while I straightened it up. I thought I was going to have to surface for a minute, but I managed to get it straightened out. By the time I did and got back over to Jeff, he—"

Even at twenty, he was too young to see a friend die, whether it was at his hand or an accident. The thought of it stopped him cold. It wasn't an act. I had seen far too many people fake emotions while I was a Military Police Officer. This was real. And because it was real, it destroyed all of my theories about who did what to whom.

I softened. "Okay, tell me what you saw. Take your time. I really need you to be as accurate as you can."

"Jeff was just floating."

Most divers had to add extra weight to a belt they wore around their waist in order to obtain zero buoyancy. That meant you didn't sink and you didn't pop to the surface. It was different for everyone. I had to carry an extra eighteen pounds. It wasn't so bad in the water, but on the beach, it was an extra burden on top of the tanks, masks, flippers, snorkel, and other assorted gear a diver carried. For Jeff to "just float," he had to have expended all the air in his lungs and replaced it with the dark, cold water of the Edmond's Underwater Park. The question was why or how had that happened.

Nelson may not have realized it, but my best guess was that he knew, even if he didn't know he did.

"What about the other diver you saw? Do you remember anything about him?"

"He was wearing a black wet suit. It was all black, like I've seen the Navy SEALs wear on television." Nelson sat silently pulling the image from the rooms in his mind, where he had already locked it away, to where he could see it again. "He had something written on the suit. On the left side. You know like over the heart." He tapped his hand on the left side of his chest over his heart. "Not words, but a logo or initials. Nothing long, just a few letters." He stood up. "It's all in the report. I told it to the cops when I came out of the water. Call them. Check it out."

He glanced around at the restaurant and its clientele. Did he bring his young girlfriend here to impress her? Maybe this was where they came after prom. Was I showing my age? Did high schoolers even bother to go out to eat after their prom? From what I'd heard in the last month, I was convinced that they left home, went to the site of the prom, had their photos made, and then headed for the nearest motel or house where the parents had too much trust and the kids had too much lust.

I stood up with him. "I've got a good idea. I know a place where they don't card. I'll buy that first round. We'll take my car and I'll drop you off at your house when we come back. That way I'm not contributing and you're not driving drunk. Deal?"

He nodded. We left the restaurant and walked across the parking lot. The smell of fish hung heavy in the air. Several boats were unloading at the docks behind us. We could hear the high-pressure hoses as they swooshed off the gutting and cleaning tables erected dockside for the use of the people who paid to keep their boats in a slip.

Leigh and I had been on several boats as guests and even spent a weekend on a forty-foot sailboat, where we and another couple planned to cruise the San Juan Islands. We left an hour prior to sunset on Friday, planning to come back late Sunday. The other guy was a well-trained sailor. I was as ignorant of all things related to sailing as I would have been to the space station, had I been invited to spend a weekend onboard, whirling around in space.

By Saturday afternoon, I was getting the hang of being a novice at the absolute end of the sailing food chain, when his girlfriend decided the time was right to tell him she wanted to start seeing other people.

We were in the middle of a very large waterway surrounded by islands, some completely uninhabited even in this modern day. The water passing beneath the boat was extremely deep and desolate. I thought that her timing was incredibly poor. She could have easily been tossed overboard and the only people who would have seen her were those in the boat as it left her to fend for herself. He didn't do that, but I was convinced that our presence on the boat was what kept him from doing so. Since then, we'd not been invited back, he had a new girlfriend, and the old one, by all accounts, was seeing other people on dry land.

I opened the door and got in on the driver's side. Nelson opened his door, hesitated a second, and then crawled into the passenger's seat. I drove to a little place just north of the Seattle city limits on Aurora. It was a section of hot-sheet motels, hookers on every corner, and bars that catered to anyone with the price of a drink or anything else that happened to be on the unprinted menu.

We went in, grabbed a table in a corner, and sat down. I sat with my back to the wall and positioned Nelson so he faced me and had his back to the door and to any stray police officer who had nothing more to do than come in and roust the bartender for serving underage patrons. If a cop walked in, I would see him first and I could pull Nelson's beer bottle in front of me.

All the way over, I had been trying to piece it together. I thought I had all the pieces to the puzzle, but a few were missing. I knew that now. I also knew that Nelson was moving down the list of those who could have killed Jeff, but I didn't want to let him off the hook just yet.

I ordered two beers in bottles from the waitress. She was in her late twenties or maybe her mid-forties. It was hard to tell. She was tall, thin, and blonde with dark roots and a scar running from the middle of her right cheek to her earlobe. She had the look of a woman who had been the target of far too many drunken backhands delivered by someone who only hit her because he loved her. She didn't wear a ring but I would have been willing to bet several had graced her ring finger and, at some point, had been stolen, sold, or pawned when times got hard. She was a walking ad for heartache.

She brought the two beers and a plastic basket lined with a paper napkin. The basket was filled with pretzels. Nelson immediately grabbed a handful and popped them into his mouth. I waited. One quick bite and he was ready to spit them out. They looked like they had been sitting on the bar since the last decade and his reaction to their taste proved it.

I chuckled. "A word of advice, my friend. In a place like this, if you don't see it opened, don't eat it or drink it." I took a pull from my bottle and leaned in closer. "Okay, let's cut to the chase. Jeff was sleeping with several of the girls in the senior class. He waited till they were eighteen, then it was legal. He promised them whatever they wanted in order to take them to bed. I'll bet he even discussed it with you. It was good for a conversation when the two of you sat around after a dive." I studied him. "How am I doing so far?" He didn't respond, so I kept going, "For Patti, it was a career in the movies or modeling. When she started sleeping with him, it cut into your sack time with her." I pulled out the computer disc I had picked up at Jeff's house and placed it on the table between us. "You ever take a computer class?"

He looked at the disc. "What's that got to do with anything?" He reached for the disc and I stopped him.

"If you're a gambling man, Nelson, I'll bet you we can find some very interesting photos of Patti and several other young ladies on this disc. And I'll bet that any number of people out there in computer land have already seen these photos." I sat back and enjoyed myself at his expense. "You know why they've seen them? Because Jeff was selling them on the Internet. I'd say Patti is already a star. She and Jeff were still going strong, and you were getting left behind. And you want to know what's really funny?"

He interrupted me by slamming his bottle on the table. "No, asshole, do *you* want to know what's funny? I couldn't give a shit about Patti." He stopped, leaned back in his chair, and placed the bottle to his mouth. Even with it there, I saw the same smile that I had seen earlier in the night. This kid was good. He knew how to transfer the flow of the tension from one person to the other. Now it was on me. He leaned forward. "You ever met Traci?"

"Jeff's wife?"

"Yeah, but now she's his widow."

The way he said it sent an alarm bell ringing in my head. "You were sleeping with Tracy?" I almost couldn't say it. Maybe he wasn't as far down the list of possible suspects as I had thought.

"Why not? He had Patti, I had Tracy. Don't you think that was a good deal?"

Now it was my time to sit back, take a sip of something, or crack some ice, and regain my thoughts. I'd handled a lot of interviews of suspects and heard some things that would make the skin crawl on an iguana, but I was totally unprepared for Nelson's revelation.

Before I could respond, the waitress came back to the table. She stopped, placed her hand on Nelson's shoulder, and gave it a gentle squeeze. It was a move to tell the customer he was special, and she was sending him a little secret signal to establish a link between the two of them. "Another round?"

She wore a skirt made of denim and a blouse that was cut low enough to allow a full view of the swell of her breasts. The skirt was so short that every man in the place, whether he admitted it or not, wondered if it was really a pair of shorts or a skirt so short as to give him an opportunity to see beneath it if the timing was right.

I nodded and, as she acknowledged me, she gave Nelson another squeeze and a look that said, "Stick around, spend lots of money, be a big tipper, and I'll flirt with you all night long and then, at closing, I'll disappear through the back door while you wait outside the front door like a dog in heat."

She was the break I needed to gather my thoughts. I tried to act as casual as I could after learning that both couples were also involved in mate swapping.

Maybe I was getting old or out of touch, but the fact remained that, no matter what else he did or who he did it with, Jeff was murdered, and I planned to find out who did it and why.

"Tracy was more than a sex partner to me. She was, I mean, I—" Nelson began.

"You loved her?"

"Yeah. And she loved me."

"And the only thing that stood between you and her

was Jeff?" He just moved to the top of the list again.

"No, Jeff didn't care about her. It was mutual. They had already planned to divorce. Killing him was not a requirement to have Tracy. I had it made. Tracy and Patti anytime I wanted either of them. Why would I do anything to fuck that up?"

# Chapter 21

I sat in my office the next morning and went over the things that had crashed on me like twenty-foot wave on Honolulu's North Shore. I felt like I was completely engulfed by the water, so cool and comforting, yet so deadly at the same time. I had two choices. I could let it take over and hope it eventually rolled me to the safety and security of the dark sand beach. My other option was to fight and conquer it. Ride the curl. Stay just on the edge of total collapse, keep my balance, work the wave, and pay no attention to the tons of water just over my head, roaring like a freight train on steroids. Do that, and do it correctly and slide gently to the shallows on my board when it was all over and start again.

I chose the latter.

My mentor when I first went into investigations with the Military Police was one of the last World War Two veterans to still be on active duty. He had been in and out of the army several times and by the time I met him he was three years away from having a cumulative total of the twenty years of active duty he needed to retire. By that time, he was in his late fifties, and he told everyone he had been around so long the army had a special pay category for him. According to him, he was the only person in the army drawing "decrepitency" pay. His age and time in the army notwithstanding, he was the best all-around investigator I ever met.

When I hit a wall, I always thought back on his philosophy, '*Look at the tree and not the forest.*' I needed to look at the trees one at a time. I opened my desk drawer and heard the door to my office open from the street. At that time of morning, there were few choices as to who it could be. My first choice was George.

"Colonel, you in there?" George called from the front of the office.

"Back here, George." I didn't want the distraction, but with George I always felt an obligation to talk to him.

When he came in, he was holding two cups of coffee. This was something he had never done in the past. I was momentarily shocked at the sight of him standing in the middle of my office, a cup in each hand that he did not get from my coffee pot.

"What's the occasion, George? It's got to be something special."

He handed me a cup without explanation and turned to sit on his usual spot on the window sill. George simply motioned with his head for me to take a seat.

"I want to help," he said as he took a sip, making "help" come out like "hep."

"Help who? Do what? I don't think I understand."

"I want to help you. Be a detective like you. You know, like you was the Lone Ranger and I was Tonto."

It was all I could do to keep from laughing until I looked at his face. There was not a line on his deep mahogany face that said he was anything but serious.

"George, I—I don't know what to say. I never thought about having a partner. I—"

"You don't have to let me in on everything you do till you know I can handle it and you can trust me. I know a lot more about the peoples what live here in town than they think I do. I can be a big help to you. You just tell me what you want me to do, and I'll do it."

With that, he stood up and walked out, leaving me to wonder just what he knew that I didn't. After the conversation with Nelson the previous evening, I wondered just how much about my town and its residents I knew.

For the next hour, I spread all the material, I had been given and collected on my own that related to Jeff's murder, on my desk. The more I looked, the more I knew I almost had it. There were only one or two pieces of the puzzle missing but they were the keys that held everything else together.

I kept going back to the inventory list of what Jeff had when he was pulled from the water. The inventory and the police report.

The police report made no mention of a third diver in the water with Jeff and Nelson. If Nelson had been without oxygen for a sufficient time, he may have been hallucinating. But what if he wasn't? Who was the other diver and where did he come from? More importantly, where did he go and why was there no mention in the police report.

I was making notes on a long yellow pad when I stopped and looked at the inventory again. I went through the list carefully. I did it a second time and a third to make sure I was not missing something. When I completed my third check of the list, I felt certain I knew how Jeff died. Now all I had to do was come up with the who and the why, and I had an idea for that as well.

The first thing I needed to do was make a dive in the water park once more before it was overrun by curiosity seekers. The police markers had come down two days ago and the weather yesterday was too bad to make a dive.

I needed a dive partner. I hesitated for a second prior to picking up my phone. It was like the receiver was on fire. I knew if I picked it up, I was going to get burned. The scars may not be immediately visible, but they would blister and leave a mark that would probably last a lifetime.

Outside my door, the traffic was moving slowly down Main Street. The parking spaces were filling with early morning shoppers heading to the stores still in business in the downtown area. Like most small towns, Edmonds had suffered the effects of shopping malls and giant stores that sold everything, except the things you needed in small quantities.

I watched an old man in a small straw hat driving a new Cadillac that he planned to park in a spot across the street. The coffee that George brought me was still hot and steam came from it as I held it and watched the old man make his first attempt at parallel parking. It took four more tries before he finally was satisfied with his parking job.

The right rear tire was off the pavement and had crabbed half way up the curb to the sidewalk. He climbed out, pushed the remote on his keys to lock the car and headed up the street to the city utilities office.

When I turned back from the window, the phone was still in my hand. I looked at it and made my decision. I listened to the number ring three times then there was a click. I thought the call was about to be answered by a machine and was half way to putting it back in the cradle when I heard a voice.

"Max, so good of you to call. I wondered when I would hear from you again." Anna's voice slipped into my ear and quickly traveled to my brain where I replayed the mental tapes of our previous meeting. I hesitated a second before responding.

"Anna, it's Max. You know, we did a dive together—"

"Max, you don't have to introduce yourself. I remember you. Quite well, I may add."

"I hope I'm not interfering with anything. I…uh…I wanted to make a dive today and I was wondering if you would be available." Was I stammering? It felt like it.

"You caught me on the ferry. We're just pulling into the Mukilteo Terminal. I can be at your office in half an hour. I have my gear with me. Will you call the dive shop and have the tanks ready when we get there?"

I could hear the engines of the ferry as they reversed and slowed the massive ship for the final glide to the dock. "I'll take care of the tanks. Do you need anything else?"

"No, I'll have everything I need today. See you in thirty."

I placed the handset back on the console and just sat for a moment. I wanted to dive the park again as a part of my investigation into Jeff's death. Actually, I needed to dive it if my hunch was right. And, if it was right, time was truly of the essence. As soon as it was reopened to the public, I knew there would be more divers down there in the next few weeks than had ever been there in the past few years. Curiosity seekers, mostly, who wanted to see where he died, or, in my case, where he was murdered.

I called the dive shop and told them I needed four tanks for a dive in an hour. I was assured they would be filled and ready. The phone sat in front of me on the desk. A call to Leigh was in order, or was it? Neither of us had placed any ground rules on our relationship, whatever that was. I had never asked Leigh if she had been dating or had gone out with any other men since we started dating. I never asked her not to, just as she had never placed the same restrictions on me. She was a beautiful woman.

I cared for her, and I felt like she cared for me in return. Why was I playing with fire? Anna was a volcano ready to erupt. When she did, it would make Mount St. Helens look like a Roman candle held by a school boy on the Fourth of July.

Did I want to be sitting on the mountain when it erupted? Before I could answer that question to my satisfaction, the front door to my office opened and Anna walked it. This time, she wore jeans and a pair of black shoes that slipped on and had no laces. Were they called pumps? I had no idea and didn't care. She wore a soft, silky-looking blouse that was brightly colored with little flowers. It was short sleeved and accented her year-round and, I imagined, all-over, tan. Her hair was in a ponytail and swayed from side to side as she walked across the room. She carried a small gym bag in her left hand.

"Max, so good to see you again." She came straight to me, took my right hand in hers, leaned in, and gave me a quick kiss on the lips. Twenty years ago that would have meant much more than it did today. I had been kissed on the lips by female acquaintances in the last few years as much as I had on the cheek. Was this one of those kinds of kisses, or did it have more meaning than I realized or wanted to accept?

"Anna, I'm so glad you were available. I know it was a short notice, but I really need a dive partner today." I still held her hand and led her to the couch where she took a seat. I sat beside her and turned to face her.

"I hope you didn't need just any dive partner. I'd like to think I'm special." Her smile was intoxicating. "Are we going back to where we were the last time?"

"Yes, I want to go there one more time before the tourists and curiosity seekers take it apart for souvenirs."

I looked up and saw George passing by my front door. He placed his hand on the door handle, ready to open it but did a quick check and saw Anna sitting on the couch. He dropped his hand, caught me looking at him, and tossed me a slight salute as he walked on his way. I almost wished he had come in and given me an opportunity to back off a little. No such luck, though.

"I hope you don't mind, but I'd like to change into my wet suit here and not at the dive shop. The changing rooms there leave a bit to be desired." Without waiting for a response, she stood. "Is your restroom back there?" She pointed to the back room where the coffee pot, refrigerator, office supply cabinet and bath room was located.

"Yes, just help yourself. I hope it's better than the dive shop. Remember I'm here by myself."

"Oh, I remember," she replied over her shoulder without looking back as she walked away. "It won't take me long to change."

Since she was changing in my office, I thought I may as well do the same. I walked out the front door and headed for my car when an Edmonds Police cruiser pulled up in front of me on the street.

The passenger side window rolled down, and I heard Gunny call my name.

He leaned across the seat to speak to me. "Hey, Colonel. Got a minute?"

I stopped, leaned down, and propped one arm on the top of the car. "Always, Gunny, what can I do for you?"

"You still looking into Coach Payton's death?"

"Off and on, I guess."

"More off or on?" he asked.

I learned a long time ago that, when someone asked a question out of the blue that didn't belong, I should be very careful in my answer.

"I have to make a living, you know, and I was doing a little looking around for Tracy, his wife. Nothing official, so no money was changing hands." I also knew not to let an open door close. "Why?"

"Just curious, is all." He paused for a second. "He wasn't as squeaky clean as everyone thought, you know?"

He had my curiosity up, so I leaned down and got as close to the window as I could to hear him.

"Yeah. You may just want to 'let dead dogs lie,' as the old saying goes," he said.

"That's an interesting statement, coming from you, Gunny, especially since he worked with your kids as well." I looked him in the eyes. "It was your daughter that he coached, wasn't it?"

As soon as I said it, I felt the window beneath my arms begin to roll up as he hit the switch. I jumped back in time to keep from getting caught in the window and as soon as I was clear of the car, he took off. Half a block away, he hit the lights and siren and pulled around a car that had stopped at the traffic light. Coincidence? I probably would never know, but unless he was wearing a Bluetooth or had psychic abilities, he did not receive a call that I had heard.

I walked on to my car, opened the back, and retrieved my dive bag. The day was slightly overcast, and we were expecting an afternoon drizzle. I'd been in the rain on every continent we had, except Antarctica, and I'd never seen rain like what fell in the Seattle area. The clouds moved in, gray and heavy laden. It got dark and, all at once, you were covered in a mist, and then the real rain started. It simply engulfed everything and everybody. One minute you were dry, and the next you were soaked. The area around Seattle probably sold more umbrellas and sunglasses than any place on Earth. You needed both almost every day. As I looked at the clouds, I figured we had time for an hour in the park before the rains came. The rain would not disturb the dive, but it meant that we would get wet getting to the park, which was no problem, and stay wet when we came back out of the water.

I carried my dive bag and opened the door to my office. As soon as I got in, I heard Anna call my name. "Max, is that you?" she called from the back room.

"Yes, I thought I'd change here as well and then we can go straight to the park." I sat the bag down on the corner of the couch, intending to wait till she had changed and then use my back room to do the same.

"I bought a new dive suit since we last saw each other, Max. It's a two piece and I really like it." She was in the back room and not in the bathroom as I had expected. I thought she would change in the bathroom, do the make-up thing, and come out.

I was looking at the open door when she stepped out. She had the zipper tab for the top of the wet suit in her right hand and he held the other side of the black suit top in her left. "I can't seem to get the zipper to work. It's the first time I've worn it. Can you give me a hand?"

The top was open sufficiently to give me an almost unobstructed view of her breasts. I didn't know if it was nature or a talented surgeon, but they were magnificent.

The glance was enough to make me want to see more. If that was her desired effect, it worked.

I walked toward her just as she slipped the two parts of the zipper together and gave it a firm tug. Her hand raised it to a point several inches from the top. "Oh, look, it caught and I could do it myself." She smiled and I could see the tantalizing look of a woman who liked to play games in her eyes. "I hate to do things myself. How about you, Max. Do you like to do things alone or with someone?" Before I could come up with an answer, she smiled again and walked out of the room. "I had better get out if you're going to change in there." She came out and sat on my couch, crossed her legs, which were now encased in the brightly colored wet suit, and leaned back. "We don't know each other well enough to change in the same room." She looked at me and added, "Yet. Do we?"

I did not answer as I walked into the room to change.

# Chapter 22

Anna and I had been in the water less than ten minutes when I found what I was looking for. I went back to the area where Jeff had died. I saw the deep rub marks on the rebar and the large pieces of cement which Nelson said had fallen on Jeff and killed him.

I had to use all of my strength to move a large piece of broken dock. As I tugged at it in the dark water, I saw Anna swim up to give me a hand. With hand and arm signals, she indicated that she would get beneath the corner of the stone and push up as I braced myself against the old dock and tried to roll it out of the way.

I couldn't help but look at her as she swam down to the sandy bottom of the park. She had bundled her hair and covered it with a dive hood. That along with gloves and flippers covered virtually every exposed inch of skin on her body. With a mask over her face and her mouthpiece in place, all that was exposed were her cheeks.

I swam down to her and placed my gloved hand against her exposed left cheek. Even with the glove on, I could feel the cold that had invaded her. I rubbed gently for a second. She stopped me by taking my hands in both of hers and pressing them to her face. I pulled my hands loose and slowly swam back to my position on the stone.

We managed to roll it over and, when it thumped into place on the Sound's bottom, I saw what I knew was the missing piece of the Jeff Payton puzzle. I swam down and gently picked it up. It had not been found by the police divers since, for one thing, they were not looking for it, and secondly, it had been covered when the stone that supposedly killed Jeff fell into place.

I picked it up and signaled for Anna to surface. We swam out of the park and came to the landing, where four other divers were getting ready to go in. Each of them was wearing an all-black wet suit with the name of the manufacturer emblazoned across the front or the back of each suit. Some were in large letters on the back others were smaller letters on the front. One even had the name running down the outside of both sleeves.

As we walked to the Four Runner, one of the divers stopped me and asked me to take a picture of the group. "We just completed our check dive, so we're all certified. I want to have our photo on the wall at the dive shop like some of the old timers."

I snapped three photos, checked the image in the screen in the back of the small camera to make sure they were all acceptable, handed back the camera, and hustled Anna into the vehicle.

"You seem to be in a hurry. Is there something I need to know, or maybe prepare for, Max?" She turned sideways in the seat as she spoke. "I have the rest of the week if it takes that long. My husband is out of town and won't be back till then."

My head was pounding. *What does this woman have to do? Give me an engraved invitation: Anna requests the company of Max as her paramour. The liaison will take place anywhere Max has the guts to take her. Gifts are not required and refreshments will be served.* "I want to check out something at the dive shop. It will only take a minute or two."

We drove to the dive shop and went inside. As soon as we entered, Ralph Peters the owner, rushed to Anna to see if he could assist her in any way. If he only knew.

I went to a board he had on a wall behind the register. It had photos of divers in a variety of poses and locations. Most of them had trained at the shop and sent photos of their first dive after being certified. Other photos were of divers in exotic locations around the world. I skipped through all of those until I found the one I was looking for. I'd had a nagging feeling for a week that I had seen the photo. I couldn't remember where I saw it until the divers at the water park asked me to take theirs.

"Ralph, can I borrow this for a couple of days?" I asked as I pulled the photo off the wall. I didn't wait for his concurrence. It was already in my bag before he had a chance to answer.

"No problem. Nobody's going to miss it. There's so many up there now that even I can't remember who they all are." He didn't even look up from his position behind the counter as he spoke. He was bending down, pulling a new Poseidon XStream Deep Regulator out of the display case. It was the newest model out and one that I had thought about getting but it would have to wait a while. At over six hundred dollars, it was a little out of my budget.

Anna eased up beside me as I placed the photo in my bag. "Is that what we came for?" She pulled my hand away and looked at the photo. "I hope you know what you're doing. I wouldn't want anything to happen to you." She placed her hand on mine and gave it a quick squeeze.

The clouds had decided it was time to turn serious as we left the dive shop. They were rolling in, dark and low, from the west. Before we pulled out of the parking lot, the rain began to fall in a relentless downpour. The drops were big and heavy. Rain in Seattle was the thing of legends and those legends were well founded.

We were driving up the street to my office when Anna turned to me. "Have you ever seen a ten carat diamond, Max?"

I was caught off guard by the question. I didn't try to answer until I stopped for the red light in front of the one dress shop still open in town. "Ten carats? I'm not sure I'd even recognize one if I saw it. I imagine that's a pretty good sized stone, though." I pulled through the light when it turned green. "Why do you ask?"

"I wanted a ten carat diamond ring. I wanted it emerald cut and set in platinum. It had to be internally flawless and a grade 'D' on the color scale." She looked straight ahead for a moment. "That means that it's perfect in every way. It's flawless, clear, and pure as a million-year-old glacier. A single one is found once in every ten thousand stones mined." She then turned back to look at me. "I told my husband that's what I wanted, and he got it for me. I wore it one night and put it in my jewelry safe. I've never worn it since."

"I don't understand what that has to do with—"

She quickly interrupted. "What it means is, when I want something, I get it."

I was pulling into my parking spot. The gravel crunched under the tires. A small puddle had formed beside my door, and I knew I would not be able to step over it when I got out of the Four Runner. I shut down the engine and turned to look at Anna. She was sitting, quietly looking at me. "And I suppose you have something in mind that you want?" I asked.

She opened the door with her right hand and touched my hand with her left. "We'll see, my friend, we'll see."

With that, she slid from the seat and headed to my office.

I ran behind her and opened the door. We walked in together, and she went straight to the back room. Because of the rain and the hurry to get inside, I left both dive bags in the Four Runner. I had a change of clothes in the office, but I knew she didn't.

I quickly ran back out to the car, grabbed both bags, and jumped over two puddles as I came back to the office.

Once inside, I set the bags down. I pulled a towel from my bag and dried my hair. I draped it across my shoulders and called to Anna. "Do you need your dive bag?" I asked as I looked at the blinking light on the answering machine on my desk.

"Yes, that will be nice. Please bring it back here for me," she called out from the back room.

My hands were sweaty when I grabbed the handle of the bag. I was playing with fire and I knew it. She was married. I knew nothing about her family life, but I got the distinct impression that it was not a happy one. Did she have children? I had never asked and I wasn't sure I even wanted to know. I held the bag and shifted the weight as I walked to the back room.

My front door was locked. The only light I had turned on when I came in was the one on my desk. It was cloudy, overcast, dark, and raining outside. Overcast in Seattle was the same as "lights out" in any other city in the world, so my office was not quite a dark room, but it was close. I walked through the opening to my back room.

Anna was standing, facing me. She had taken her dive suit off. Both pieces of the suit lay folded neatly on the floor. The shoes she wore from the dive sat beside the pile. Anna was silhouetted in the partial darkness of the room. She had a large towel wrapped around her. I recognized it as one I had used several times when Leigh and I went to the city pool. It was tucked in, covered her breasts, and fell to just above her knees. She was a stunning sight and took my breath away.

My eyes feasted on her face, her hair, her body. My mouth refused to work and my tongue felt as if it was permanently attached to the roof of my mouth.

Anna took her left hand, reached beneath her right arm, and pulled at the point of the towel which she had tucked in. As she pulled, she stretched out her right arm. Her hand motioned for mine. I gave her my hand and the towel fell to the floor.

"Say one word and you'll never see me again," she said and then covered my mouth with hers, making it impossible to say anything even if I had wanted to.

# Chapter 23

Anna left at ten p.m. the night before. She had to catch the last ferry or we would have stayed together all night, I was sure. Or maybe I just hoped. I didn't know if it was good timing or not, but Leigh left for her sister's house in Dallas two days before I made the dive with Anna. Leigh would be back in three days. Would my life be back to normal by then?

I had what I needed now to close the books on Jeff Payton's murder. And I knew it was a murder, not an accident. He had been killed, and Nelson didn't do it. A couple of more calls were in order, and then I could put this one to bed.

The roads were still wet from the rain the previous evening as I left my apartment. I had one stop to make before I went to my office.

There were two police cruisers parked in front of the Treetopper when I pulled into the parking lot. One was from Edmonds, the other from Seattle. The greasy spoon restaurant was on the King County line, so it was not unusual to see a Seattle P D or sheriff's department vehicle parked in the lot.

I parked beside the one that was combat parked. The driver had backed the cruiser into the parking space. That way, if he needed to get out in a hurry all he had to do was drive forward. No backing and turning was necessary. All military vehicles were supposed to be parked that way. *Old habits die hard*, I thought as I walked by the cruiser and opened the front door of the restaurant.

I looked around for half a second and spotted Gunny sitting in a corner booth. He was positioned so that his back was to the wall and no one came in or left without his seeing them. I was not an exception, so he waved as soon as he saw me. "Hey, Colonel. Come on over. We're just getting started on the war story portion of the meal." He moved over so I could slide in beside him. He nodded to the other two officers sitting across from him. "That's Miller." A young man probably just out of the academy offered his hand. "And the ugly one with the mustache is Dunnigan."

Before I could say anything, the officer he introduced as Dunnigan who was wearing a Seattle Police Department patch on his shoulder like Miller, leaned across the table. "Ugly? You old fart, coming from you, that hurts." Dunnigan turned to me. "I've been on the Seattle PD for the last ten years, and I've had to put up with him all that time. We play poker once a week." He extended his hand. "Glad to meet you. Do you play poker?"

I nodded. We ordered breakfast and, throughout the meal, the conversation went from poker, to the Mariners, to the weather, and finally to the lack of attractive hookers working along Aurora. That was the main drag through the city and the place where a john could get anything, up to and including, a case of bubonic plague from a hooker.

"Okay, gentlemen, and I use that word with caution when I speak about Gunny, we have to pay up and leave. Duty calls." Dunnigan stood and nodded to his young partner. "Your turn to pay. Right?"

"If it gets paid, it's my turn," he said as he pulled out a twenty and walked to the counter where the waitress waited behind the cash register. She took his money, counted out the change, and waited patiently for a tip.

He placed the remainder of the twenty in her hands and walked toward the door.

"See you guys later." Dunnigan walked a step then turned. "And the offer to play poker is open. Any Wednesday. We rotate the locations so the cops don't find out." He laughed at his own joke and walked out the door, his partner close behind.

Their exit left me alone with Gunny.

"I think I'm going to add some things to the police report on Jeff Payton's death today, Gunny," I said.

"Really? What's that?"

"I think he was killed. Not by accident." I waited for a response.

Gunny placed his coffee cup on the tabletop. "The other choice is intentional. That would be murder. Is that what you're saying, Max?"

"At first, I thought it was that kid, Nelson, who was diving with him, but then I started looking into Jeff's background and found some very interesting things." I leaned closer in order to whisper. "I found out Jeff was taking some photos of some of the girls at school, and—"

Gunny quickly leaned in to me. "That's probably not something you want to start spreading around town. He was a well-respected coach. Not many people are going to believe—"

This time I interrupted him. "I'm not asking anyone to believe anything. I've got the proof. I found an album in his garage and a box of negatives."

"What kind of negatives?"

"I haven't had a chance to go through them yet. I've just held them up to the light, but I can tell you that he had quite a collection of nudes. Some of them look pretty young."

Gunny sat back for a second. "I can't believe that. He was one of the most respected coaches and teachers the school ever had." He looked out the door with what the army called the two-thousand-yard stare. It was the look a soldier got when he couldn't handle the demons or when it had been too long since his last clear thought. It could happen in an instant or it could take days to bring it on. He shook his head, as if to clear it, and stood up. "I'll get breakfast." He dropped fifteen dollars on the table. That came to about a six dollar tip. "When do you plan to turn over the negatives?"

"Sometime this morning. I need to go by the office and pick them up, and then I'll bring them by the PD." I stood beside him. "Why don't I meet you there? I'll tell Fitzgerald that you convinced me to bring them in. There may be something in it for you."

We walked out together, and I watched Gunny get into his car and pull out of the parking lot. I followed behind him and kept him in sight till he turned west and headed toward town.

I took another route and drove to a Starbucks just over the county line. It was a free-standing building with a large parking lot so I picked a place behind the structure and parked. I walked around the building and entered through the front door. As soon as I got inside, I was immediately quizzed about what I wanted to drink by a guy who was entirely too happy for that time of morning.

I ordered a plain coffee and he seemed disappointed that it was not something more exotic, but he pulled the black handle on the coffee brewer, filled a large cup, and called it by an Italian name.

It took an hour to nurse the cup and read the Seattle Times. I read the comics, found out what was playing at the multi-plex at the mall, and read my fortune for the day. It called for me not to venture into deals where money or love was concerned. Fortunately, it said nothing about murder.

I left the coffee shop and drove straight to my office. I made one phone call on the way on my new cell phone. I'd had it a week or so and was just getting used to all the new features. My last one was one step above the first edition "brick" that could be used as a weapon as well as a phone. This one even had a voice recognition feature where all I had to do was touch a place on the screen and call out a name. Once it decided who you wanted, two more touches and the call was placed. I'd still rather drop a coin in a pay phone, but you could hardly find one anymore.

I'd been in my office less than ten minutes when the door opened and Gunny walked in. He came through the outer office and into my office.

I stood when he came in. "Gunny? I thought we were going to meet at the police department?"

"I thought I'd save you the trouble of taking the negatives over there. I can do it for you. After all, I'm the one who will probably get stuck doing the inventory." He stood in front of the desk, his hands hanging loose by his side.

"Well, gee, Gunny, I don't know. I mean, I've got this album and a box of negatives—"

Before I could answer, he unsnapped his holster and pulled his service revolver. He reached for the box I had placed on my desk with the album and the negatives in it. He reached for the box. "I really hate to do this, but I can't let you take those photos over there."

"You might want to take this with you, too." I held my hands in front of me and pushed aside a stack of papers I had on my desk which uncovered a piece of white plastic in a frame. The plastic was similar to a White Board, but this one had a frame around it and a long cord looped from one edge to the other. It was a diver's slate meant to be worn around the neck so divers could communicate underwater. If you needed to say something, you wrote it on the slate, tapped your partner on the shoulder, and he or she read it and knew what you wanted. "When I looked at the inventory of Jeff's dive gear, I knew something was missing, but I couldn't put my finger on it. Then Nelson mentioned writing a message to Jeff and getting an answer. The slate wasn't a part of the inventory. I went back to where Jeff died after the crime team finished. I looked around and found it about fifty meters from the site. Fortunately, the water or the bottom hadn't erased what was written on it." I picked it up. The writing was facing down. "You want to guess what it says, Gunny?"

Gunny held the pistol steady. "That son of a bitch was screwing teen-aged girls from the school. He deserved to die."

"But it wasn't up to you to do it. And he didn't need to die the way you did it—"

"I did a traffic stop on him one night. He was drinking and I wanted to give him a break. You know, the football coach and all, but I had to check his car. I got to the trunk and found an album in it. I opened it and found all those pictures. He begged me to let him go, so—"

"Let me finish," I said. "You saw the photos and found a way to pick up some extra money. For the last two years, you've been blackmailing Jeff so he could keep taking photos and having sex with some of the girls. Jeff wasn't breaking any laws. All the girls were over eighteen. He was smart that way." I flipped over the slate. Four words were printed in black on the white surface. I turned it toward Gunny. "Look at that and then look at this." I slid a large manila envelope toward him. "'You're a Dead Man,'" I read off the slate, and "'HOLD FOR MAX,'" on the envelope. "Look at the "D" and the "M". They're the same on both of them."

"This is all bullshit. You can't prove a thing." He leaned down and pulled a small snub-nosed pistol from an ankle holster. It was called a "throw down." All cops carried one. It was unregistered and likely had no serial number. In case of a questionable shooting and a weapon couldn't be found, a throw down was dropped and the record showed the perp had a weapon and the shooting was justified. Or he could just shoot me with that gun, and there would be no way the bullet could be traced back to Gunny.

He held the throw down in his left hand and his service revolver in his right. "I'm about to come in here and find you dead. Maybe a jealous husband who did it. You have a reputation, you know. Could be a client who was not satisfied with your work."

"I saw the receipts. I know Jeff was paying you and I know he stopped. I think he finally figured out that he had nothing to lose, except his job and, in the long run, it was financially worth it."

"Do you know one of those girls was my daughter? I didn't know till one day I went to his house and saw a photo. I just saw her face but that was enough to know who it was. Another photo was lying on top of it. If I'd seen her nude, I would have killed him on the spot and not waited."

"If I hadn't seen the dive team photos, I would have never thought about you, Gunny. I saw the divers when they pulled Jeff out. There were three, not four. One team went into the water and you came out with them."

I was on a roll and felt good about how I had come up with Gunny as the killer, but he didn't share my enthusiasm. I heard him pull the hammer back and cock the pistol.

Then I played my trump card. Before arriving in my office I had made a stop at the Edmonds Police Department. I went directly to the detectives' room and knocked on Fitzgerald's door. It was open so I gave a good rap on the door frame. I knew he heard me, but he ignored me for longer than I was prepared to wait. I walked in and pulled the door closed behind me.

He looked up from his busy work. "What the hell do you think you're doing?"

I took it as a small power play. Had he stood up, I would have been more concerned.

"I have some information on the Jeff Payton murder that you don't have."

"Jeff Payton drowned in a diving accident. End of story." He put both hands on his desk. In body language class that indicated something along the lines of him saying, "I don't believe you but tell me more."

I sat on the edge of the one chair in his office. "No, it wasn't an accident. It was made to look like one, but if you'll be in my office in about twenty minutes, I think you'll get some information you may find of interest."

"Max, if you have information on a murder, you give it to me right this minute, damn it." Now he was either mad or very interested because he stood up.

"What I have is about ninety nine percent of the puzzle. If you're there, you'll get the same new pieces I do when I get them." I stood and looked around the room, making sure he saw me do so. I took a deep breath to add emphasis to what I was about to say. "And you may be surprised at who gives us the remaining pieces."

Fortunately, Detective Fitzgerald arrived at the office about two minutes in front of Gunny. It was a cheap trick used in every movie ever made, but it had worked for me once before when I had a major who was selling army food from a warehouse at Fort Benning. He implicated his sergeant so, when I interviewed the major, I had the sergeant in the back room. As soon as the sergeant heard his name mentioned, he came out of the room and gave me all the information I needed. I wanted Fitzgerald there just to listen. He did just that and heard everything he needed to hear.

He stepped out of the room with a Glock 40 in his hand and pointed it at Gunny. Before he could even say a word, Gunny turned, ducked, and fired. He hit Fitzgerald just above the belt buckle. Fitzgerald grabbed his midsection and crumbled onto the floor.

As soon as he fired, I rolled across my desk and tried to pull open a cabinet drawer where I kept my pistol. Gunny saw what I was doing and fired a shot that barely missed me. I felt the desk splinter as I scrambled to get some distance between him and me and regain some sort of hold on the situation.

Why I heard it, I'd never know, but I actually remembered hearing my front door open as my hand closed on my Colt Model 1911. I thumbed the safety off and fired twice at Gunny. As soon as I did, I rolled back to the corner and placed my hand on Fitzgerald's wound. He was pumping blood and there was no way for me to stop it and protect both of us from Gunny at the same time.

Gunny had moved behind the wall in the back room. "Colonel, I don't want to do this, but you're making me. All I wanted was that no good bastard dead. I wanted to do it, and I wanted it to be slow, and for him to know who was doing it."

I couldn't see him but I could fire through the walls and take a chance. I saw his shadow fall across the floor, backlit by the overhead light in the room. As soon as I saw him extend his hand and slide halfway around the door frame, I prepared to fire. That's when I heard three shots fired in rapid succession. Every weapon I had ever fired had its own signature. Once you heard it, you never forgot it. A Model 1911 pistol like I had in my hand sounded completely different from a Glock 40, or an AK-47, or a .30 caliber carbine, or anything else.

The sound I heard was a small caliber, and it was fired in a pattern that suggested it was a revolver and not an automatic. Three shots and then all was quiet.

The office was as quiet as if we had been inside one of the Pyramids of Giza. There was the distinct smell of cordite in the air from the gunpowder that was left behind when any weapon was fired. The silence after a firefight was unlike any other. It was a time when the participants took stock of their lives. We asked simple questions in that nano-second of silence. *Am I alive? Am I wounded? Can I move all my limbs? Are my balls still intact? Did I tell my wife or mother or girlfriend or whoever, that I loved them the last time we spoke? Did I buy my Dad a Christmas present? I don't want to die having him think I don't love him.* All of that required less time than it took for my eyes to blink or my heart to pump enough blood to my brain for me to react.

I was about to turn toward the sound when I heard Gunny's weapon drop from his hand. My instinct was to continue my turn toward the new shooter. I had one hand on Fitzgerald's wound and the other one extended with the .45 in it. I tracked the sound and found myself pointing my weapon at a man in a brown suit. He was standing in my outer office near the front door, and he held a small chrome plated pistol in his hand. It took a second for it to register.

"George, is that you?" I still covered him with my pistol.

"It's me, Colonel. You okay?"

"I'm fine. Call nine-one-one while I keep the pressure on Fitzgerald's wound." I looked at Gunny. He had fallen forward and was laying half in and half out of my back room. He still held the throw down in his hand. He had blood covering his left shoulder and a small round hole almost dead center of his forehead.

We were less than four blocks from the main fire station, so I heard the sirens of the EMT vehicles as soon as they pulled out of the station.

George stood over Gunny. "Please tell me that policeman was trying to kill you, and I did the right thing by shooting him."

I had scrambled to the back room and picked up the towel that a day earlier had graced Anna's body and was now soaked in blood as I pressed it to Fitzgerald's stomach.

He was still conscious, and I talked to him in an effort to keep him that way. He motioned for George to come to him. When George leaned down, Fitzgerald spoke to him in just above a whisper. "You did the right thing. I saw it."

George stood and said the most prolific thing he probably had ever said in his life, "Colonel, we got's to keep that man alive."

By that time, the EMTs were rolling a gurney into the office to take Fitzgerald to the hospital. Several city police officers came and when they saw a dead fellow officer and the chief of detectives wounded, their immediate reaction was to arrest both me and George and give us the needle on the way to the lock up. Fortunately, Fitzgerald was coherent enough to explain that we were not to be arrested before he succumbed to the pain and the drugs administered by the EMTs.

It took three days to sort it all out. Fitzgerald was kept in a drug-induced coma for two days. On the third day, he collaborated the story both George and I told to the other detectives. A later interview with the dive team that answered the call to the underwater park the day Jeff was killed confirmed that there were two divers who entered the water, but both men remembered seeing Gunny in a wet suit with tanks at the park.

George told me he had come by the office to show me his new suit and to let me know that he had decided that he was ready to train with me to become a private investigator. He had applied for a concealed weapons permit and had gotten it earlier in the week. The pistol he shot Gunny with was an old Smith and Wesson .32 caliber, just as I had thought during that instant of time when I was running on instinct.

Leigh came home, and she and I had dinner together at a new restaurant on Lake Union. All through the meal, I felt like something was wrong. Had I forgotten to shave? Did I wear a blue shirt with green pants or vice versa? After dinner, we moved to the bar. The restaurant had an incredible view of the lake. The skyline of Seattle sparkled in the night sky like a hole had opened in the darkest part of the universe and all the stars had congregated in one place. But, still, something was wrong.

"Is everything okay?" I finally asked as our second drink arrived.

Leigh was unusually quiet and, when I asked, she just looked at me. "How many times have you been shot at?" Before I could answer, she added, "No, no, how many times have you been shot at and hit and how many times have you shot back and hit somebody else?"

There was no answer that would work, and I knew it instantly. I turned and looked at the lights from the restaurant as they danced across the water. Each ripple made them dance even more.

"Shot twice. Maybe three times. I'm not sure about

the last one. It could have been just a piece of debris that nicked me."

"The question had two parts," she almost whispered.

"Some things you don't keep on a scorecard," I answered with some difficulty.

She reached over and took my hand. "I could never be an army wife and I don't think I can continue to be a detective's girlfriend." She stood up. "I'll get a cab home." She leaned down, kissed me, and placed her finger against my lips to keep me from saying anything.

It was almost midnight when I left the restaurant. I needed to clear my head after talking to Leigh. I took my time as I drove north on I-5, took the exit to Edmonds, and drove slowly into town. At first, I was going to go straight to my apartment, but the closer I got the less I wanted to be there. The only alternative at that time of night was my office.

The yellow crime scene tape had been taken down and the cleaners had done a good job of removing the evidence of my having had a dead man in my back room and one bleeding out in my office.

I had one message on the machine. The light was blinking in the dark as I had not turned on any lights when I came in. I walked to the cabinet, opened the bottom drawer, and pulled out a bottle of Jack Daniels. I didn't want to get drunk, and I couldn't say I need to drown my sorrows. I wanted to cut through the pain. All the pain, the pain I felt and the pain that I had caused. I downed about an inch in a small water glass and set the glass by the still open bottle. The light was still blinking, so I hit the play button and listened.

"It's probably too late for you to get this message tonight but if you do, remember what I said about my sleeping alone." It was Anna.

I wouldn't call her tonight, but I knew I would at

some later time. Some night when it was dark and I was alone with too many memories. Not tonight, but some night.

I poured another drink and sat alone in the darkness.

## THE END

## About the Author

Paul Sinor is a published novelist and a produced screenwriter. The first book in his latest novel series was published in March of 2015. His other published works include one novel and a book on marketing screenplays. Eight of his screen plays have been produced as feature films, and he currently teaches screen writing at the University of West Florida in Pensacola. He has a MFA in Creative Writing and is a member of the Mystery Writers of America.

Sinor is a retired US Army officer and spent five years as the army liaison to the television and film industry in Los Angeles where he worked on such films as *Transformers 1-3, GI Joe, I Am Legend, The Messenger, Taking Chance* and numerous television episodes.